Marginally Yours

LAYLA NOX

Published by Layla Nox

Copyright © 2025 by Layla Nox. All Rights Reserved.

Cover by Disturbed Valkyrie

ISBN Paperback: 979-8-9930320-1-6

No part of this book may be reproduced in any form or by any electronic or mechanical means, including information storage and retrieval systems, without written permission from the author, except for the use of brief quotations in a book review.

This books is a work of fiction. Any names, characters, places, and events are products of the author's imagination or are used fictitiously. Any semblance to actual persons, living or dead, events, or locations is entirely coincidental.

Any references within this work of fiction that is trademarked, including any works, products, brands, or companies, are not authorized, associated with, or sponsored by the trademark owners.

Contents

Content Warnings — vii

Chapter 1 — 1
Chapter 2 — 8
Chapter 3 — 16
Chapter 4 — 25
Chapter 5 — 32
Chapter 6 — 39
Chapter 7 — 44
Chapter 8 — 52
Chapter 9 — 60
Chapter 10 — 71
Chapter 11 — 78
Chapter 12 — 87
Chapter 13 — 95
Chapter 14 — 101
Chapter 15 — 107
Chapter 16 — 115
Chapter 17 — 121
Chapter 18 — 129
Chapter 19 — 137
Epilogue — 141

Acknowledgments — 145
About the Author — 147

For those who haunt the earth, waiting to feel alive again. For those who begged for freedom and had to scratch and claw for it themselves.

Content Warnings

This story deals with some sensitive themes. Please read carefully and prioritize your own mental health.

Anxiety, Assault, Choking, Death of a Parent (off page), Depression, Graphic Language, Indentured Servitude/Captivity, Kidnapping (off page), Mental Health, Murder, Sex in Public, Sexually Explicit Scenes, Unprotected Sex, Violence

Chapter One

I grew up in this bookstore. When I was a kid, my parents would bring me here once a week to pick out a new book from the used section in the back. That all ended when they split up and Dad moved across the country with his new girlfriend while my mom and I pinched pennies in a town whose claim to fame at the time was not one, but *two* dollar stores within a half mile radius. With the closest library being nearly an hour away, and Mom working overtime to pay bills, I resorted to making up my own stories. I had just hit double digits at the time, so I'm sure they were terrible, but getting lost in the world I was creating was even better than getting lost in someone else's.

The problem with having a brain that only functions when you're pumping it full of serotonin is that finishing a big project isn't really in the cards most of the time. I'd get an idea, do all the research, plan and plot and outline, and then lose steam and move on to the next bright idea.

There are fewer worse fates for a creative person than having either ideas or motivation, but not both.

I continued to jot down bits and pieces of stories

throughout my preteen years but eventually gave up around tenth grade. I never lost my love of reading, though. If anything, that passion only grew over the years. I figured that if I couldn't create an epic fantasy world, I could at least be an enthusiastic participant in someone else's.

Daring heroes going on wild adventures in expansive fantasy worlds, rescuing the downtrodden, overthrowing tyrannical dictators, and freeing the people from their oppressive regime... There was so much to immerse myself in that the real world didn't seem so bad anymore. The only way I was able to forget about all the bad shit going on around me was with my nose in a book.

Between the messy divorce, the gnawing ache of inadequacy, and the standard trauma associated with growing up weird in a small town, my youth was less than pleasant. As I entered my teens, this was all exacerbated by the unholy trinity of mental illness - depression, anxiety, and ADHD. My life isn't terrible, but some days I'm barely a willing participant in it. I'm here, but I'm just so *tired*.

Eventually, I found a new way to jump into different worlds when I discovered single-player RPGs, and it wasn't long before I was spending more time outside of reality than in it. I started growing out my hair and cut it to look like one of my favorite video game characters. Long on top, pulled back into a dark brown knot, and buzzed short on the sides. Then came the beard, short and thick with a slight red tint.

This was followed by the next logical choice, of course. Most of my spare cash over the years has gone towards covering myself from shoulder to fingertips with a collage of tattoos from my favorite books, movies, and games. I have some more personal ones that are hidden, but I decided that, if I'm going to spend the time and money to get them, they should be visible, and anyone who has an opinion about it can eat shit.

In a small town like ours, this all means a lot of judging looks from people who have known me to be generally quiet and polite my whole life, and a severely limited list of local career prospects.

Lucky for me, a medical research team opened a new facility just outside of town a few months after I graduated high school. They prioritized hiring locals, and they didn't care what any of us looked like, as long as we were ready to work. They're environmentally responsible as far as anyone can tell, and they offer a pretty sweet benefits package. It's a great gig, and it pays really well.

I was one of the first security guards they hired for their surveillance team when they opened. I'm a bigger guy, and while a lot of it is muscle, most of it is just tacos and genetics. I figured they hired me because my bulky 6'4" frame is more than a little intimidating, but it's really just a desk job. Because they went to such lengths to make sure that they weren't pieces of corporate shit, there's very little pushback and not much risk of break ins, which makes my shifts a breeze, but a little dull.

So, I read.

I keep all the camera feeds visible and have the volume up on the motion sensors around the building, but I'm barely involved. I'm just a body in a seat, ready to act if there's an emergency, but otherwise just taking up space. In my head, though, I'm fighting Balrogs and solving murders and being swept up in epic adventures and romance.

My favorite place to get my fix is this bookstore. It's conveniently located on my short drive to work. There's always parking right out front, and I might as well have a "Devon's Parking Only" sign installed. Hannah in the café makes the best coffee I've ever had in my life. Some days, I'll grab a new release that I've been waiting for or pick something from the

"Staff Suggests" table. Other days, I'll grab an old paperback from the used shelves behind the stacks.

I'm easy to please, so I'm rarely disappointed by anything I read. If I can escape into the book, I'm happy with it. Fantasy is my preferred genre, but I love a good murder mystery or historical fiction, too. Contrary to the male reader stereotype, I've also been known to enjoy a good romance.

Today's goal is a new release that I've been excited to read for a while. It's a continuation of a series I read as a teenager, with powerful dragons and brave riders going on an adventure to fight the looming evil and free their people.

A frigid wind gusts down the street, biting at my ears and tossing dead leaves around my feet. Pumpkin carcasses lay forgotten on the doorstep, left out after Halloween for the squirrels and birds. I hurry through the door to escape the cold. The chime of the bell on the door is so familiar, ingrained in my brain like a Pavlovian trigger that releases all my tension.

Eddie is behind the counter, and I wave at him as I make my way to the display. We went to high school together and his uncle worked here before he retired, so he made sure Eddie got the job. I'm glad, because he's always been a friendly face, even though we were never really close. He returns the wave and goes back to what I can safely assume is the crossword puzzle from today's paper.

I pick up a copy from the table and turn to take it to the register, but a flash of purple in the stacks catches my eye. There's a woman standing in the used books section, pulling books off the shelf and scribbling something on a clipboard before gently sliding them back and repeating with another book.

In a town with barely a 4-digit population, it was rare to see a person that you hadn't known your whole life. It's completely unheard of to see a beautiful woman, presumably your own age, who you don't at least already know about.

Yet, here she stands, a modern miracle.

She tucks a few stray strands of her pale blonde hair behind her ear, securing them with her pen. Her hair is loose and short, falling just below her chin, with wavy bangs framing her heart-shaped face. Her pale blue eyes dart across the clipboard and a lavender sundress flows around her as she turns away from me and heads to the next shelf. She's got tiny fine line tattoos scrolling across the nape of her neck and down into the back of her dress, and I'm overwhelmed with a desire to trace them. *Stop it, you fucking creep.*

She continues her task, and I watch for a few minutes while I build up the nerve to... do... something? I can't think of a single valid set of words that I can string together to introduce myself to this girl. I don't think I've had to introduce myself to someone new in a decade, honestly. What do I even say? I try to brainstorm for a minute, but it's more like a brain-sprinkle because all I can come up with is 'Hi, I'm Devon'. I already want to punch myself in the face on her behalf.

My brain is still buffering, trying desperately to come up with something to say, when I realize in horror that I've been staring at her this whole time, and now she's looking back at me. How long have I been staring?! I panic, and the spinning wheel of awkwardness in my head settles on "Smile and Wave", so that's what I do. I'm positive the smile has too many teeth, and the wave was more of a salute, but some kind of merciful deity grants me relief when she waves back, her smile crinkling the edges of her eyes.

Success thaws my brain enough to come up with a few words to say, but shock delays the response time just enough that she's already turned back to her clipboard when I hold the book up.

"Have you read this one yet?" I ask. Generic, but it was the most non-invasive thing I could think of to ask someone who's actively employed at a bookstore.

Unfortunately for me, whatever grace I had been granted has been snatched away. Disappointment floods over me as she moves farther down the shelf with no response. She doesn't even look my way.

Message received, loud and clear. I may have mumbled a bit, but I'm only a few feet away. Either she doesn't have any interest in talking to me, or she's busy and doesn't want to be disturbed. Regardless, I'm not keen on being an unwanted intrusion, and I can respect her space. She's probably just busy.

I head up to the register and Eddie stuffs the newspaper under the counter when he sees me coming.

"Hey, Devon," he starts, and my disappointment must have been clear on my face, because he gives me a questioning look. "Dude, why do you look like someone kicked your puppy?" Eloquent as ever.

"Oh," I huff out a laugh, schooling my face back to indifference. "I'm good. I was just trying to talk to that new girl and I think I interrupted her." His lips turn up, and I guess that I'm not the first person to try talking to her. I go on defense, adding, "I wanted to see if she'd read this yet." I set the book on the counter, and Eddie's smirk becomes a full-blown laugh.

Now I'm annoyed. I know he can see it on my face because he scrambles to recover.

"Sorry, man. I don't mean to laugh at your pain," he says, still laughing and clearly not that sorry about it. *Asshole.* "Was she looking at you when you were talking to her?"

My brows furrow, and I think for a second. "No," I reply, even more confused. "She was looking at her clipboard. Why?"

"Dude," he says with a chuckle. "She didn't ignore you. She's deaf."

My mouth hangs open for a moment while I process the

information. I'm an actual idiot. Obviously, I don't know anything about this girl yet, but her smile and wave would imply that she's at least polite enough to have acknowledged me talking to her.

"Well, not completely deaf, but mostly," he continues. "I think she said she's got like twenty percent hearing or something? Her name is Callie. She just moved here a few days ago. Today's her first day. She does talk and she can read lips pretty well so it's not a big deal if you don't know any sign language or anything. She said she'd teach me some while she's working here, too. She's really nice." He continues rambling about her while he rings up my book and takes my card. "She likes to read anything from romance to fantasy as long as it's fiction. She's a year younger than us. She walks to work and she's..."

I hold up a hand, stopping him from spouting off any more facts. We end most of our conversations this way, so he's not offended. Usually, I do this because I've reached my quota of Eddie infodumps for the day, but honestly, I'd just rather learn all of this straight from the source.

"Thanks, man," I say with a laugh, grabbing my bag from the counter and heading for the door. "I'll see you in a few days."

I reach for the doorknob, but a tingling sensation stops me. It feels like static electricity shooting down my spine. I spin around, but it's gone just as fast as it came. My gaze lands on Callie again, still deep in concentration in the stacks. I'm considering going back to talk to her now that I know she wasn't ignoring me when she catches me staring *again*, and I lose my nerve. She gives me another cheery wave, and I give her an awkward one in return before scurrying through the door like a coward.

Chapter Two

I make it to work in record time, and I'm barely in my seat before my phone is in my hand, desperately searching for any nugget of information on this girl. Social media is a menace to society, honestly. I feel like a stalker, but I need some kind of opening to talk to her, and I'll take any help I can get.

As long as it's not coming from Eddie, anyway. I like the guy, but he's a little overwhelming sometimes.

All I have is a town and a first name to go off of, but at least it's not a super common name. *Callie.* I check Eddie's friend list first and find nothing. Maybe she knows someone here and that's why she chose such a dreary, unappealing place to move to. I type her name into the search bar alone, hoping maybe there's a mutual friend that makes her pop up. No such luck. I add our town to the filter, and it shows similar name matches only, so maybe she didn't update her location yet. I add the bookstore to the workplace filter and get nothing at all.

Ok, so she might just not be on social media. Not a bad

thing, just inconvenient. Guess I'll have to do this the old-fashioned way.

I spend the next hour trying to focus on my book, but I only make it about five pages in before I give up and flip between doomscrolling and mobile games for the rest of the night. The next day, I consider stopping in again but decide against it. The book I got yesterday was huge, and there's no way I could have finished it in one shift. I got a head start on it this morning, and I'm planning on finishing it tonight.

My grand plan is to stick with the original idea and ask if she's read it yet. Eddie said she was into fantasy books, so I'm guessing there's at least a 50/50 shot that she has. If she hasn't, I can recommend it to her, and if she has, I can ask her what she thought of it and ask her for a recommendation for my next book. It's not much, but it's a start, and it's an easy conversation for her to escape quickly if she's not interested in talking to me.

I spend my entire shift reading and finish the last page about 10 minutes before it's time to go. Leaving work at four in the morning is annoying, but driving through the empty, peaceful town is relaxing. The drive is short, and I pass out as soon as I'm out of my uniform.

—

I usually don't remember my dreams for long after I wake up, but I'm still thinking about last night's dream on my way to the bookstore.

I was walking on a mountain path somewhere I'd never been, low-hanging clouds covering the peaks in the distance. I could see the little town at the base of the mountain that the path was leading me to, but I couldn't make out much detail. There were wooden cabins and old-fashioned stalls with cloth awnings, and I could hear the chatter from the people milling about. I could hear people talking just behind me, but as soon as I turned to look at them, I woke up.

It's been a few hours, but I can still see everything clearly. I considered going back to sleep, wondering if the dream would pick up where it left off, but I'd *definitely* be late for work. I'm already cutting it close, and I need enough time to chat with Callie.

I head to the café first, waving at Eddie on my way in. I zero in on her immediately, and I remind myself that I'm supposed to be at least pretending that I'm cool, so I focus on chatting with Hannah while she makes my coffee.

Callie's wearing a black t-shirt with what might be a metal band logo hidden by the front of a pair of worn denim overalls. She wheels a cart full of books through the used section, sliding them into their places on the shelves. The top of her hair is pulled back into a little bun like mine, and the rest hangs free. She plucks a pen from the front pocket of her overalls and a clipboard from her cart.

I make a show of picking up a book from the display table and reading the synopsis while she checks things off on her clipboard. I've already read this book. Twice, actually, but she doesn't need to know that. I position myself so that I'm facing her but keep my eyes down, watching her only from my peripheral vision.

As soon as I catch her looking my way, I set the book back on the table and "accidentally" catch her eye. *How serendipitous*. She gives me that wide smile again, and I grin back.

Now's my chance.

She sees me walking towards her and she doesn't freeze or look around for an escape, so that's a good sign. I'm at least a foot taller than her, and a security uniform isn't much of a reassurance of character these days.

"Hey, welcome back," she says, and her voice is lower than I expected, and maybe a little too chipper. She's probably just giving me her customer service voice because I'm accosting her in her workplace, but damn it if it didn't send a thrill through me that she remembered me. She sets her clipboard on the pile of old hardcovers. "Is there anything I can help you with?"

"Yeah, hey. I'm, uh, Devon. I'm here a lot, as you can tell. I, uh, went to school with Eddie," I mumble awkwardly, mentally kicking myself. *Stop saying "uh", you dense motherfucker.* This is not going as smoothly as I'd hoped. She's squinting at my mouth, and I remember she's not just listening but also reading my lips. I consider holding out a hand to shake but remind myself that this isn't a business deal and my palms are probably sweating, so I stick one in my pocket and point the other at the display for the book I just finished. I clear my throat and try again.

"I just finished that one last night. Have you read it?" My words come out with a little more confidence this time, and hopefully I'm loud enough for her to hear without struggling. I'm now standing at the proverbial fork in the conversational road.

The knots in my stomach loosen a bit when she nods emphatically and says, "Yes! I just finished it the other day. I loved it!" I can feel my shoulders loosen up, and I realize just how many muscles have been clenched as I release them. I hope she can't tell that I'm slowly melting back into a human being shaped puddle of anxiety.

"It was so good," I tell her, running my hand over my beard nervously. We chat about the book's pivotal ending for a few minutes. We both thought it was really great and agreed that it was left open for another book on purpose, even though nothing has been announced.

"Oh shit," I mutter, glancing at my watch. "I have to get going or I'm gonna be late for work." Her face falls just enough for me to clock it and I almost feel bad being excited about that. *Almost.* I decide that a few minutes won't kill me. "Hey, I need something to read tonight at work. Any suggestions?"

She lights up again, and I'm three seconds from calling off tonight. She lifts her clipboard a bit and pulls out a book, holding it out to me. I can tell it's an early 80's fantasy just by the cover. It's mostly lime green, with a big technicolor illustration of a dragon in the middle, a tiny rider perched on its back. I could have sworn that pile was all hardcovers, but this is an old paperback with worn edges.

"This series was always one of my favorites," she explains. "It's a little dated but the story is great. There are like 25 books in the series, too. It's a classic dragon fantasy, so I think you'll really like it." The last word is clipped, and she pinches her lips together like she's trying to make herself stop talking. She looks down at the floor. "I hope so, anyway," she adds quickly, quieter than before.

Holy shit. Is she *nervous*? To talk to *me*? There's no fucking way.

I wrap my hand around the book and wait for her to release it, but she's still holding on tight, staring at my hand. "I bet I will," I reassure her quietly, and then I remember that *she can't fucking hear you, dumbass*. So, I rustle up every ounce of audacity I own and gently touch the fingers that she has clamped around the book with my free hand. Just a light brush against the backs of her fingers, and that drags her attention back to me.

"Oh," she squeaks, letting go of the book. *Great, too much.* "Ok, let's get you checked out so you're not late." *Or maybe not?* I can't tell, but she's still smiling while we get to the register.

I don't tell her that I'm already late at this point because I honestly couldn't care less, but I hurry behind her anyway.

"I'll start on this when I get to work," I tell her as she rings me up. "I'll let you know what I think next time I stop in, but I'm sure I'll like it if you do."

She beams at me and slips my receipt in the book before

handing it over. I slide it under my arm and turn towards the door.

"See you later," she calls after me.

I make sure I turn to her before I speak this time. "Absolutely," I tell her with an awkward little wave that makes me want to cut my fucking hand off. Then she gives me the exact same wave back and I could probably get hit by a bus right now and die happy.

What the fuck is happening? I don't think I've ever been this nervous in my life. I mean, I haven't spent much of it talking to beautiful women who are into fantasy books *and possibly me*, but still. My cheeks hurt from grinning like an idiot for the last 20 minutes. My palms are definitely sweaty, and I think I might be shaking a little bit.

That went... good. Like, really good. Most importantly, she was definitely just as anxious as I was, and I don't think it was in a bad way?

Oh, shit. *Was* it in a bad way? I hope she wasn't just being nice to me because I was a customer, and she had to. *She's not flirting with you, idiot. She's just hot and talking.* Fuck. Next time I go in, I'll wait for her to talk to me. If she actually wants to, she'll ask me about the book.

I spend the drive to work replaying the entire interaction, analyzing her reactions and agonizing over whether I made her nervous or uncomfortable. I'm aware that there is a huge difference between the two, and I have absolutely no interest in making her uncomfortable.

I roll into work about ten minutes after my shift starts and apologize to John for making him stay late. He waves me off without a word and hustles off before his wife calls to chew him out. I sit at my desk with my new book. I'm still rolling our conversation around in my mind and self-flagellating over it when I open the book and the receipt slips out.

I think my eyes actually bulge out of my head when I

notice the 10 digits scribbled on the back in glittery purple ink. Underneath the number, she wrote "in case you finish the book early" with a little smiley face.

I don't know how long a human being can go without breathing, but I'm definitely setting a record.

I have no idea when she had the chance to write this. I must have been staring at her face so hard I didn't even notice her hands. What I do know is that she had to have done it after I touched her hand, which means I've been torturing myself for nothing. I can't even bring myself to be annoyed about it because *holy shit, she gave me her number*.

I save her number in my phone immediately but stop myself from texting her just yet. I need to read a little bit, and then I'll start the conversation with something to report. That feels like a solid plan.

Two hours later, I'm about 100 pages in and I'm invested. This is pretty good, honestly. I think I've read enough to give her an honest update, so I stick the receipt in the book to mark my page and pull out my phone.

> Hey, it's Devon. I'm about a third of the way into this book and it's pretty good. Excellent suggestion, thank you!

Perfect. I set my phone down and go back to reading. I don't expect a response right away. She's probably still at-

My phone vibrates. It's been maybe 30 seconds. I don't think I've ever grabbed my phone so fast in my life.

> Good, I'm glad you like it! Who's your favorite character so far?

> Definitely the dragon.

> Lmao that sounds about right. It's a short one so you'll probably finish it tonight. Do you want me to see if we have the second one in stock?

> That would be great, thank you! What about you? Who's your favorite?

> I'm also pretty partial to the dragon.

We chat back and forth for a while, some replies coming immediately and some taking a while until around six when I assume she leaves work, because I get a steady stream of quick responses for the rest of the night. We mostly talk about the book, or other books, which is fine with me. I give her live reaction updates, and she sends me teasers of spoilers without actually telling me anything useful. I'm just about done with the book when she tells me she's heading to bed, and I realize several hours passed in what felt like two and it's past midnight. She makes me promise to send her a final update when I'm done so she can read it in the morning.

I'm in the process of texting her back when she sends me a selfie of her lying in bed holding up a pinkie and smirking at the camera.

My brain short circuits and the only response I can come up with is a selfie with my own pinky out, followed by "Pinky promise. Goodnight."

Oh, I'm so fucked.

Chapter Three

I wake up to multiple texts from Callie.

I finished the book after she went to bed last night and sent her my thoughts on it. I told her that the characters were well developed, and the plot had a good mix of action and romance, definitely enough to keep the interest of both types of readers. I thought the main character was a little too righteous and she could probably loosen up a little, but overall, I liked it.

Then I sent her a selfie, the book spread open in my hand to the last page with an overdramatically sad face. I was going for "effortless and adorable", but I deleted the first 38 attempts, and the vibe is decidedly more "goofy".

I almost unsent it, but I had to commit to the bit eventually. I followed it up with one more text before leaving work.

> Not sure how I'm supposed to sleep after that cliffhanger but I'll see if I can manage to survive until tomorrow. I'll come in a little early so we can talk about it if you have time. Goodnight, Callie.

She texted me back at 7am. Of course she's a morning person. She's basically made of sunshine.

> I'm so glad you liked it! I'll have the next one set aside for you when you get there. I'm sure Eddie can manage without me for a little bit lol.

> Also, I found another one you might like. I'll set a copy aside for you.

> If that's ok, of course. If not, it's totally fine!

> Ok I'm probably blowing your phone up so I'll leave you alone and stop yapping now.

> Oh, and good morning!

I don't know if cuteness aggression is a thing in people like it is in animals, but I feel like I need to bite something in half. She's just a little ball of anxiety too, huh? I feel so seen.

I rush through getting ready, making sure I at least smell nice, and my hair and beard are neat before I leave. It's hard to look good in a security uniform.

I really need to stop in on my day off next time.

I leave an hour early, and I have a feeling it still won't be enough time. When I get to the bookstore, Eddie is at the register. He pats a hand on a small stack of books, presumably the ones that Callie had set aside for me and dips his head towards the café with a suspicious smirk.

She's sitting in one of the chairs with two cups on the table in front of her and her face in a book. She's so invested in whatever she's reading that she jumps when I pull out the chair across from her.

"Oh, hey!" She beams at me and slides one of the cups across the table. When I cock a brow at her, pink flushes her cheeks. "I figured you'd be in a hurry so I asked Eddie what you normally get but he had no idea so I asked Hannah what she normally made you and that worked but then I realized I wasn't sure exactly what time you'd be here and it's been a while so it's probably already cold so I was just going to grab another one when you got here but..." She takes a deep breath in and holds it for a moment before letting it all out in a long, slow huff.

"Sorry, sometimes I forget how to people and I just ramble away," she mumbles, and reaches for the cup. "I'll be right-"

I wrap my hand around the cup before she can take it, but she doesn't see it and ends up wrapping her tiny hand around mine. Steam puffs up out of the vent as our hands collide, and it might be coming out of my ears, too. I had planned to make a big show of drinking it and telling her how delicious it is, but every thought in my head has been replaced with a fucking mariachi band, so it's a solid ten seconds before either of us says anything.

"Thank you," I finally say, and it takes every iota of willpower I have to pull the cup out of her grip and take a sip. "It's perfect," I tell her, taking another and watching her over the cup.

It actually is, but Hannah has been making me the exact same caramel macchiato for almost 2 years now so I would hope so. I won't tell Callie that, though.

Her relief is a palpable thing, and I can actually see it wash over her face. "Ugh," she says, blowing out a relieved sigh. "Okay, good. So, you liked the book?"

I let out a quiet laugh because she's asked me if I liked it about 743 times in the last 12 hours, but I'm trying really hard not to make her anxious.

Well, *more* anxious, anyway.

"Yeah, for sure," I reassure her. "I really liked it. I'm excited for the next one too. I bet I'll finish it tonight." I had already looked it up and, despite being a fan favorite, it's even shorter than the first.

"Oh, definitely. I can't wait to hear what you think!" Her smile is genuine, and I don't know why I'm surprised to find that she actually wants to hear my opinions. No one even lets me talk about books, let alone gets excited about it.

We chat for a while about the next book, and then another series we both love. She occasionally looks up and down the street through the front window, and her eyes dart to the door every time the bell chimes, but I chalk it up to being new in town and nervous. She's passionate about reading, and it's obvious that she especially loves books about strong women who save the day on their own in any genre. She's especially drawn to books featuring intelligent women who outwit their opponents.

As we talk, I can feel something forming in the back of my brain. An extraordinary woman who thinks she's nothing more than ordinary. She finds out what she's capable of through a series of trials and finally learns that she's been someone important all along.

It's just the tiniest trickle of inspiration, but the familiarity of it, mixed with the excellent company, has me grinning like a fool.

We finish our coffee and reluctantly part ways. I promise to text her live updates while I read tonight, and she's already plotting out my TBR list.

We repeat this process at least once a week for the next few weeks. I stop by the bookstore for our afternoon coffee dates, she sends me on my way with a new book or two, and then we spend the evening texting. I've noticed that she's a little closed off about her personal life, but she's more than happy to go on about books. Anything I've read, she's also read and has an opinion about. She's been slipping up lately, though. She'll start to share something and then cut herself off. I don't want to pry, but I wish she'd open up more.

Sometimes, I bring my notebook with me to work and jot

down some ideas for my story. It's mostly just stray thoughts and a basic outline at this point, but it's something. I haven't told her about it yet, but I will. Eventually.

Today has been a routine coffee date day. We're wrapping up our conversation so I can head to work when an idea hits me. So far, we've only hung out at the bookstore. I'm not complaining, but I'd like to see her outside of my uniform and without having to keep an eye on the clock the whole time.

"Hey, do you work Saturday?" I ask. She shakes her head, and I take it as a sign from whatever patron saint watches over anxiety-riddled nerds. "Do you maybe want to go out with me that night? There's this place in the next town over where you can get really good food, but it's also got this cool little arcade in it." She doesn't answer me right away, and the panic starts to settle in. "Only if you want to, though. It's just a fun place, and we can talk about books when you're not on the clock and..."

I'm rendered fully mute the second she reaches across the table and grabs my hand. In the weeks that we've been hanging out, this is the first time she's touched me on purpose.

My eyes drift back to her face, and she's got one side of her mouth pulled up in a mischievous smirk. She knows I'm about to word vomit, and she's having fun watching me squirm before letting me down easily. There's no way she isn't laughing at me in her head.

"Sounds fun," she says finally, cutting off the Self Deprecation Express barreling through my brain. She still sounds a little wary about it, but she gives my thumb a tiny squeeze and I decide not to question it.

"I don't drive, though. Would you be okay with picking me up? My apartment is right up past the square." She tilts her head toward the little topiary display up the street, and I know there's a row of apartments behind it. There are only two apartment complexes in town, and the other is an absolute shithole, so I assumed it was that one. I consider making a lame joke about her living in the topiaries, but it hits me that she's comfortable enough to both tell me where she lives and let me drive her, so I decide to keep it to myself.

This time, anyway.

"Yeah, absolutely," I tell her, like I'm not about to spend all day Saturday detailing my car now. "Text me your unit number. I'll come get you at 6?" She nods, her smile so wide it's almost touching her ears. I glance at the clock again and swear. "Ok, cool. I really do have to get going now though, or I'm gonna end up getting written up. Or beat up, probably by John's wife, if I make him late getting home again." We both chuckle at that, and she leads me up to the register.

With two new books in hand, I'm sliding into my car when I glance at the front window. Callie is standing in the corner watching me. When she realizes she's been caught, I can see her cheeks flush from the sidewalk. She gives me a sheepish smirk but doesn't move until I'm gone.

By the time I pull into the parking lot, I've got a new text.

> Don't mind me, just enjoying the view.

Fuck.

I walk into work with a few minutes to spare, and John gives me a silent nod of approval as he leaves. I barely notice him, my brain still processing the text. *Don't mind me, just enjoying the view.* Excuse me? Is she enjoying my suffering, or just trying to put me into an early grave? How do I even respond to that without sounding like a creep?

Although, she was the one staring at my ass through the window.

I cycle a few responses through my head before settling on one.

> Thanks, I'll be here all week. Happy to be of service. 😊

I follow it up with a gif of a guy in a tux bowing on stage and I'm rewarded with a laughing emoji. A few minutes later another message arrives.

> We just got a huge shipment full of used books so I'll be sorting those for the rest of the night. Please please please still send me your thoughts on the book. Just wanted to let you know that I might be too busy to respond right away.

> No problem, do your thing. I'll talk to you when you're free.

That gives me some time to blow through these books, although I'd rather be talking to her while I do it. The first is a hardcover, another installment in the dragon series that she got me hooked on. The second is a small paperback that I've never heard of, but I recognize the author. He's a fantasy legend, and he's known for writing a series with a million different semi-standalone books that all connect in little ways in the end. It's a little beat up on the edges, but otherwise in good condition.

I settle in for the night and start reading, but I notice that some of the pages have writing in the margins. It looks like a purple fountain pen, scrolling across the page in neat, curly handwriting. There are tiny dots in some places that definitely look like accidental ink drips. I flip through a bit more and realize it's not on just *some* of the pages. It's *most* of the pages. There are notes about the characters, definitions of words, some underlined quotes, and even some ideas on what the author could have done differently.

Did Callie do this? Her number was written in purple

pen, but it was glittery and a brighter shade of purple. I pull out my phone to text her and remember that she's busy tonight. I'll ask her later. I slip the first book back into my backpack and start on this one, making sure to read all of the annotations as well.

An hour or so later, I'm a quarter of the way in and I'm already obsessed. The book is great, but the comments are even better. Some of them are funny, others insightful.

There's a point early on in the book where the main character has to make a choice, and the annotator took up every spare inch of the margins on both pages to write out what they think would have happened if they made the opposite choice. Don't get me wrong, the author's choice was logical and well-written, but it was an interesting take. The annotator's idea would have taken the story in a much more intense direction, and this book is meant to be lighthearted, but it was definitely something to think about.

The darker path gave me an idea of my own, though. I abandon the book for a bit and pull a notebook out of my bag, jotting down some ideas. Once I've got my thoughts down on paper, I sit back and finish the book.

I don't think I want to dive into the other book just yet, so I review my handwritten notes from earlier and add on to them, fleshing out the idea a little more while I'm still inspired. I think back on the dream I had the other day. A group of adventurers coming down a mountain to a little village hidden between the peaks. Then the idea that I got when I was talking to Callie, about a woman who has to learn that she's strong.

As soon as my pen hits the paper, it's like opening a floodgate. I fall into the familiarity of writing and, before I know it, my replacement is here to relieve me for the morning. I stuff my notebook back into my backpack and clock out, but my brain is still running through the outline that I have almost finished. This is further than I've ever made it without dropping my focus, and I can't lose momentum now. I get home and pull my notebook back out.

It's almost 6 in the morning when I finish my outline. It's basic and definitely needs some research before I start actually writing, but it's a finished outline. It's something I've never done before, and all it took was someone else's comments scribbled in the margins of an old book.

I was so engrossed in writing last night that I never even took my uniform off before I sat down. I strip everything off and lay down. It dawns on me as I'm plugging my phone in that I never texted Callie at all last night. *Fuck*. I send her a message now, so she doesn't think I completely ditched her.

> Hey, I'm sorry I didn't give you any live updates last night. I actually spent the night writing instead of reading. Going to bed now. I'll tell you more later. Goodnight!

Hopefully she's not mad. She seems like someone who would understand getting lost in inspiration when it strikes. I set an alarm before I roll over and fall asleep. I dream of a girl with pale blonde hair dragging me by the hand through a mountain pass, and I've never slept better.

Chapter Four

I'm so used to working the night shift that I usually don't even bother with an alarm, but today I slept in so long that I almost don't have time to stop at the bookstore.

Tomorrow is our date. Is it a date? So far, every conversation we've had has screamed "friend zone", so it's entirely possible that I'm imagining any real connection beyond friendship. If it *was* meant to be a date, it's probably not anymore.

I only had one text when I woke up, and it was just a vague 'okay, goodnight!', so now I'm itchy all over and worried that she's upset with me. I'm aware that it's illogical and that she's probably not mad, but unfortunately the little gremlin in my brain only knows the words "you", "fucked", and "up", so I need to lay eyes on her to confirm she doesn't hate my guts now.

I rub at the center of my chest as I walk toward the front door, trying in vain to relieve the tightness there. Callie is working the register, so she's the first thing I see when I walk through the door. Her face lights up when she looks up at me, and suddenly the tightness vanishes.

"Hey," she calls, giving me a little wave from behind the counter. "How'd your writing session go?" She's smiling, and literally nothing about her demeanor indicates that she's annoyed with me in any way, but my stupid brain is still not convinced. She curls an eyebrow at me, and I realize that I've just been standing here staring at her like an idiot, reveling in the fact that she didn't spit in my face when I walked in.

"Oh, uh..." I shake my head lightly, running my fingers through my beard. "Sorry, I had a late night. Writing was actually really good. That other book you set aside for me was actually..." I pause as Eddie barges through the office door and takes a seat on the stool next to her. I don't feel like explaining the annotated book to him, so I switch directions. "...really good. You got any other suggestions for me for tonight? I woke up late, so I don't have much time to browse."

The words fall out of my mouth before I remember that I still have a whole book to read from yesterday, but she doesn't seem to notice the mistake.

"Oh, yeah!" She gives Eddie a questioning look and he nods solemnly. As soon as she turns, he shoots me a wry smirk as if he's doing me a favor by allowing her to step away, despite the fact that I'm literally the only customer in the store. He means well, but sometimes I want to kick him in the head.

Callie brushes past me and it takes all of my frayed self-control not to grab her hand as it bumps into mine. Then she glances at me over her shoulder with a look that screams mischief. "Right this way," she almost whispers. Wait, did she touch my hand on purpose? Was I *supposed* to grab her hand?

Fuck, I am so bad at this. I have *got* to chill out. I'm going to scare her away before I even get the opportunity to make her fall madly in love with me.

I follow her to the used books and try not to drool on myself or something equally creepy since that seems to be my default mode with her when there's not a cafe table between us. Apparently, all of my brain cells keep rushing south with the blood flow. I watch quietly as she scans the stacks and jam my stupid hands into my pockets before they get a mind of their own. This was decidedly *not* the correct move, because it pulls the rough fabric of my uniform painfully tight, and the friction sends a shock straight to my spine. I groan quietly, slowly removing my hands from my pockets and fisting them at my sides.

"Aha," she shouts, and my heart stops. *Oh shit, she caught me.* I whip my gaze to hers and *thank fuck* she's staring at the book in her hand and not my current... situation. "Whoops," she whispers, leaning closer to me. I look around pointedly at the empty bookstore, about to tell her about the zero people who care about her yelling, but she's currently close enough that I can smell her floral perfume, so I make the smart decision to shut the fuck up before she moves away again.

"Okay, here it is." She takes a half step closer to me and holds out the book. "I love this book and it's another quick read so you could probably blow through it tonight." I'm busy trying to breathe as deeply and quietly through my nose as I can, so I don't realize she's waiting for me to take it until she grabs my hand and places it on the book. It feels like I'm touching one of those plasma ball toys, electricity zapping my skin wherever she touches it. Is that what she feels too? She stays there, her hands sandwiched around mine and the book, eyes locked with mine for what feels like eternity.

Plot twist, it was like ten seconds.

Her lips turn up slowly, and she gives my hand a light squeeze. "I'll be free tonight if you want to talk about it." She is most definitely not mad at me. Her hands are *still* wrapped around mine, her thumb ghosting back and forth slowly over my knuckles. This is the most embarrassingly chaste thing that has ever left me with a hard on in my entire life. Thank fuck for thick fabric slacks.

I need to start carrying around a spray bottle for myself. *No, bad dog. Stop humping the furniture.*

I take a deep breath that shakes off the paralysis and wrap my free hand around hers. I'm definitely grinning like a psychopath with way too many teeth, but I can't help it.

"Thanks," I say in an exaggerated whisper, making a show of looking around cautiously for imaginary patrons we might be disturbing. She rolls her eyes at me, but the smile stays plastered on her face. "Unfortunately, I do have to get going," I tell her. She sticks her bottom lip out in a pout, and I want to bite it. *Damn it, where's the spray bottle?*

"As much as I'd love to stay and hang out, you have work to do and I enjoy having kneecaps, which I will most likely not have if I come in late again."

"I suppose that's fair," she says with a laugh. Then I shock us both and reach up, brushing my fingers against her cheek before sweeping a stray hair behind her ear. I feel like I licked a defibrillator paddle. By the stunned look on her face, I think she does too. If I don't get out of here now, I'm never going to leave, but I'm feeling inspired to be a little bold today for some reason. Instead of taking my hand back, I cup the side of her jaw and swipe my thumb across her cheekbone. She visibly shivers, her eyes darting back and forth between my eyes and my mouth.

"I'll pick you up at six," I whisper, and then turn on my heel and strut up to the register. Eddie is never going to let me live this down, and I can't even bring myself to care.

It is *definitely* a date.

I'm so distracted by whatever that was that I almost forget to check the book for those little purple scribbles. I thumb through some of the pages in the middle and find nothing but plain black print. Despite the last fifteen minutes, I can't help but feel a small flash of disappointment as I hand the book to Eddie. I glance behind me while he rings it up, desperate for one more look at her before I go. My gaze finds her immediately. She's standing right where I left her, her finger running across her cheek right where mine had been a few minutes ago. She's looking in my direction, but her eyes go straight through my chest, a faint smile playing at her lips.

She must feel me staring at her because she looks up suddenly, her cheeks flushing when she realizes she's been caught. *Oh, this is going to be fun.* I arch an accusatory eyebrow at her, and she huffs, glancing around the store before sticking her tongue out at me and following it up with a middle finger.

I think I'm in love.

I send her a quick text as soon as I get in the car.

> Hope you enjoyed the view.

When I get to work, I see that she responded with another middle finger, in emoji format this time. I stick with the emoji theme and send her back a kissing face. A bolder choice than I would normally make but I'm feeling brave. I'm getting settled at my desk when her reply comes in.

> Keep it up and I will definitely kick your ass at the arcade tomorrow. No mercy.

> You couldn't reach my ass if you tried, you little troublemaker.

> Watch me. Spite is a powerful motivator.

> Looking forward to it.

I'm beaming like an idiot, resisting the urge to kick my feet and giggle at this point. We flirt back and forth for a bit before I finally take out my new book. I take my notebook out with it, just in case I get some ideas. I almost drop the book when I flip it open to see that familiar purple ink scrawled on the first page.

I know I wasn't particularly thorough when I flipped through it earlier, but there was nothing on any of these pages. Now, almost every page is written on. The ink is bright purple, bold and clearly visible. There's no way it was a trick of the light, and definitely no way I just missed them. Maybe it was some kind of weird invisible ink or something?

Curiouser and fucking curiouser.

I'm not one to look a gift book in the mouth, though. I flip my notebook open to a fresh page before sitting back in my chair and starting the book. The reappearing ink situation is weird as hell, but there has to be some explanation for it that I just can't think of at the moment.

Callie and I text back and forth throughout the night while I read, and I consider asking her about the writing. Would she think I'm insane? Or is she the one behind it? Once is a coincidence, but this is two books in a row that she's given me with the same annotations.

No, I'll wait until after our date. At least then I'll have had one good date with her outside of the bookstore before she runs screaming.

By the end of my shift, I've finished reading the book and also managed to finish tweaking my outline and start my first draft. I was feeling particularly inspired tonight, and I think my story is really developing. I've got some character descriptions and backstories written out with rough sketches of them in the margins. I'm not much of an artist, but I'm particularly proud of one of them. The blonde woman from my dream, clad in riding leathers and a fur-trimmed cloak, twin swords strapped to her back and a smirk on her face that tells the world she's survived purely out of spite. Someone recently told me it's a powerful motivator.

I don't spend too much time thinking about why she's my favorite.

By the time I get home, I've got another dozen pages or so written and I finished reading the book. I strip down and curl up in bed, setting an alarm just in case. I want to be up early tomorrow, so I have enough time to get the panic attack out of my system before I pick Callie up for the arcade.

Tonight, I dream of a battle. I'm in that little wooden village, but it's a bloody hellscape now. Brutish men slash at us with worn swords and corner us against a flaming building. We're surrounded, barely hanging on by a thread, when the blonde woman comes up behind the horde. With a dagger clasped tightly in each hand, she sneaks up behind the bandits two at a time before sinking a blade into their throats. They fall silently, one by one, and half of them are bloody heaps on the ground before the rest even realize she's there.

Now that her cover is blown, she tosses the daggers into the ground before me and pulls a longsword from a sheath on her back. She takes on the remaining bandits with expert strikes, moving so fast that they can barely keep up. I yank the daggers from the ground and come in behind the horde to assist, and we clear the battlefield together.

She's strong and fast and more skilled than I could ever hope to be. She wipes a hand across her bloody face, and I can't help but think she's the most radiant creature I've ever seen. Like an avenging angel. She takes a step towards me and graces me with a blinding smile. She opens her mouth to say something, but I wake up just before the words come out.

Chapter Five

I'm lucky I set an alarm, because I definitely wouldn't have woken up in time to get ready. I feel like I really did fight in a battle last night rather than just dreaming of one. I had planned on deep cleaning my car, but I barely manage to toss the trash and wipe down the dash before I run out of steam.

I head inside to trim the sides of my undercut and clean up my beard before hopping in the shower to soothe muscles that shouldn't be sore. The fun part begins when I start digging for something to wear.

She's only ever seen me in my work uniform, so hopefully she's into "nerd casual". I pull on some jeans and one of my favorite black t-shirts, and then a long sleeve button up. The shirt has a graffiti print of Gandalf on it in white, and the button up is black and dark green plaid. I neatly roll the sleeves up to my elbows and head back into the bathroom.

I examine my reflection with more scrutiny than I'm used to. I've never particularly cared what I look like to other people, but I find myself wondering what Callie thinks of me. Most of my long hair is pulled back into a bun, with a few shorter strands hanging down in the front. My beard is neatly trimmed, but there are some patches that are discolored, some stray strands that stick out no matter what I do.

I run my fingers over my too-wide nose and trace the dark bags under my eyes. I'm already starting to get lines around my eyes. All the things I see now used to be just *things*, but when I hold them up to the light that spills off of Callie, my brain is suddenly putting them firmly in the *flaw* category.

This is as good as it gets, I suppose.

I've got thirty minutes or so before I need to leave, so I grab my notebook and get some writing in. My outline is as done as a work in progress can be, and I've already started on the first draft. I wrap up the second chapter before I leave.

By the time I pull up to her apartment, I could probably power the whole town with the nervous energy coursing through me. I head to her door and shoot her a text on the way to let her know I'm here. She texts back that she's on her way out, so I lean on the railing and look around while I wait.

There's a row of apartments here, all connected into a single, one-story building with their own doors and little stoops. While the rest of the doors are plain, hers has a little lavender and pine wreath hanging inside the screen door and potted flowers all over the stoop. It's really not a big town, but I don't even remember this apartment being up for rent. She must know a landlord in town or something.

She opens the door, and her eyes go wide as she takes me in. I'm about to start squirming under her perusing gaze, but then she smiles, and relief washes over me.

"Well, look at that," she muses. "A scholar *and* a gentleman." I chuckle and hold out my elbow for her. She links her arm through mine, and I walk her to the car, releasing her to open the door. Once she's in, I close the door for her and take a few deep breaths while I walk around to my door. When I slide into my seat, my stomach flips when I see that she's already smiling at me.

"So," she starts, fidgeting with the hem of her dark green sweater. "Have you been to this place before?" I see her leaning forward out of the corner of my eye and realize the angle is hard for her to read my lips, so I turn the radio down and twist my head as far as I can in her direction without taking my eyes off the road before replying.

"Yeah, a few times," I tell her. I glance over to make sure she got that. Her smile tells me she did, and that she appreciates the effort. I look back at the road but keep my face angled toward her as I continue. "The restaurant has always been here, but they added the arcade about a year ago. I went there with some friends for their grand reopening event, but it was so crowded that we didn't stay long. We came back a few days later and had a good time though."

My eyes drift back to her like she has her own gravitational pull. She's got her elbow propped against the window with her head leaning into her open palm, and she's just watching me. The look on her face tells me she couldn't care less where we're going. She's just happy to be here.

"So, where did you live before here?" I ask, hoping that maybe she'll be more likely to open up outside of the store. "Somewhere close?" She shakes her head, and I almost expect her to leave it at that.

"No, I was in Maine before here. I move around a lot," she tells me. I'm guessing she sees the worry in my face at that, because she lets out a soft 'oh' before she continues. "I'll be here for a while, though. I don't think I'll be moving again any time soon."

I hide my sigh of relief under a laugh. "Good," I tell her with a sly smirk. "You can't leave until I show you the Seven Wonders." She crinkles her brows at me, and I laugh again.

"The Seven Wonders are what we call the only fun things

to do around here," I explain. "Someone started calling them that when I was in high school and it just stuck, I guess. First, we have the trail at the park. It's kind of icy around this time of year, though. It starts at the back of the duck pond and it's pretty easy to walk, but it spits you out at the top of a cliff with a really nice view of the rest of the park."

Her eyes light up at that, and I immediately know where we're going next time.

"Next," I say, holding up two fingers. "We have this really nice gazebo in the park with these huge flower bushes everywhere. Everyone goes there to take pictures for prom and engagements and shit. It's really pretty. But a lot of people also just go there to hang out and read or study or have picnics when it's nice out."

"That sounds so fun!" She's definitely excited, which is good, because I'm already formulating this entire tour date in my head. I hold up a third finger.

"Next, we have the best Mexican restaurant in town. Well, the only Mexican restaurant in town, but it's still amazing. The food is authentic and absolutely delicious, but more importantly, it's dirt cheap. I'm talking dinner for two, have to be removed from the table by crane, won't need to eat for a week kind of full. For under twenty bucks. It's always packed but they put heaters out on the patio for winter so we could still go, even if it's cold-"

I try to stop, but the words are already out and now she knows I'm already planning it. "If you want to, that is," I say, trying to recover. I chance a look in her direction, and she's looking at me like she won the lottery.

"Oh, definitely," she says, gleaming again. "Tacos are my favorite food on the planet, honestly."

Thank fuck. And then, before I can stop myself, and because I'm an actual moron with no social filter, I jump directly back into the fire.

"Okay, it's a date." I cringe, expecting silence. I beg the universe for enough luck that maybe she wasn't looking at me when I said it, but I know she was. That was so fucking dumb. Too much, too soon. This isn't a date, we're just hanging out. I can't just assume that she's interested in me because she's nice to me and we're hanging-

She says something, and my ears hear it, but my brain doesn't process it. A featherlight touch on my cheek yanks me out of my head. My eyes dart to her and she's settling back in her seat, her smile stretching from ear to ear. Did she just kiss my cheek? Is that a real thing that just happened? The neurons in my brain are running around with fire extinguishers right now.

I realize I'm frozen and she's about to start regretting her decision so I recover as fast as I can. I still don't know what she said, but I'm hoping it was something affirmative. "Awesome," I say, and then take the safe route and continue my list.

"So, where were we?" I scrunch my face up a bit, trying to rewire whatever part of my brain just fried itself.

"Four," she says, and I nod.

"Right, number four. Well, four is actually the bookstore. People really like the café, even if they don't come in for the books." She scowls, her eyebrows pinching together, and I swear it's the most adorable thing I've ever seen in my damn life. I can't help but laugh, and she realizes that her face moved of its own accord and lets out a soft giggle that I can feel in my spine. Oh, I'm so toast.

"Yeah, I know, right? At least pretend to read something," I muse. "Anyway, next is the dog park. It's not part of the actual park, and it's really small, but it's fenced in, and people usually just let their dogs go off leash and play. So, it's basically like a free petting zoo. There are some benches and stuff to hang out on, too. Not a great place for picnics, though, as I'm sure you can imagine."

"Well," she counters. "I'm sure it's a great place for picnics if you're a dog."

"Yeah, you got me there," I laugh.

"Okay, so we've got the trail," she says, holding up a finger. "The gazebo, the Mexican place, the bookstore, and the dog park." She holds up another finger for each. "Two more. What's next?"

"Six is honestly everyone's favorite. After the tacos, of course. It's only a block from the bookstore, too. It's called-"

"Strikers!" she shouts, and then clamps a hand over her mouth. I laugh and confirm her guess. "Sorry," she mumbles. "I've seen the sign, and I want to go but I didn't want to go alone. I *love* bowling."

"Well, I have excellent news for you. My cousin owns Strikers." Her face lights up and all I can think is *what a great way to go blind*, so I decide to push for a few more kilowatts. "I bet if I asked him nicely and promised to reset the machines when we're done, he'd let us come in after closing one night for a couple games." I glance at her again, and her eyes are wide.

"Yes, please," she practically begs, as if that wasn't my idea of the best night ever.

"Okay, I'll see if I can work my magic," I promise. "Now, the last wonder is mostly a spring and fall thing, but they're open all year. There's this farm that used to just sell to the local grocery store, but they decided to open their own store on the property like 10 years ago. They have fresh fruit and baked goods and packaged meat in the store, all grown and butchered on the farm. In the spring, they do these 'pick your own' events, where you can come buy a basket and pick your own blueberries or strawberries or whatever is in season. Then, in the fall, they do pumpkins and sunflowers and apples. It got really popular in the last few years, so now they do tours through the fields, and this meet and greet with the cows thing."

Oh, *that* caught her attention.

"Devon, are you shitting me? Can we pet the cows?" I can tell she's lived in cities for most of her life by the level of shock in her question. I think it's the first time I've heard her swear, too, and it gives me a twisted sense of satisfaction.

"We can, in fact, pet the cows," I laugh, and I imagine this is what she looks like on Christmas morning. "You can take pictures with them, too. They've got an old Polaroid camera, and they'll take your picture for a dollar."

"That's it," she says with finality. "We're going."

"Anything you want," I murmur as we pull into the parking lot.

Chapter Six

"So, I guess this place is like the eighth wonder, huh?" Callie walks in front of me, staring up at the neon sign in front of the arcade.

"Yeah, I guess so," I chuckle. When we get to the building, I reach over her head to push the door open, and we step into the lobby. I point a finger back and forth between the two glass doors in front of us. "What do you want to do first? Food or games?"

She hums, tapping a finger to her chin. "I think we should work up an appetite first. Unless you're hungry now?" I'm starving, but I could probably subsist on her company alone at this point, so I gesture to the door with ARCADE on it.

As soon as I push the door open, we're blasted with a barrage of sounds, from people to music to electronic game beeps. Callie is practically vibrating with excitement already, her eyes darting from game to game, and I realize she probably has no clue just how loud it is. I touch her elbow, and she draws her attention back to me.

"Hey, it's really loud in here, so I might not be able to hear you very well," I tell her. "If you can't get my attention or can't find me, just text me." She nods and follows me to the quarter machine. I pluck a plastic cup from the top of the machine and hand it to her, pouring some quarters into it as they come out of the machine. She's absolutely beaming, eyes darting around at all the different games. I fill my cup with the remaining quarters and she's still watching me, unmoving, so I wave my free hand in a wide sweep.

"After you," I mouth, and she wraps her hand around my wrist with much more strength than I anticipated before bouncing off to one of the games she had been eyeing. There are a lot of newer games here, but this one is a classic, all 8-bit pixels and high-pitched beeps. It's a one player game, so I hold her cup for her and watch. I'm not sure which of us is having a better time, honestly.

She finishes her first game and manages to make it on the high score list. At the very bottom, but still pretty impressive. She types in CAL as I hold out my hand, another quarter in my palm. "Do you want a turn?" she asks, taking a step back.

"Oh no, don't mind me," I tell her, my mouth twisting into a sly look. "Just enjoying the view."

Her cheeks flush and she turns back to the game to hide it, but the illuminated game screen just makes it more obvious. She must realize that, because she shoots me a quick look of indignation before swiping the coin from my hand without meeting my eyes and plays another round.

Two hours later, we've played almost every game in the arcade. I'm honestly impressed by her arcade skills. We both got a few high scores on different games and definitely worked up an appetite. I'm about to suggest that we go grab some food when a voice from behind us calls out my name. I spin and find the voice is attached to Brendan, a friend from high school who I barely talk to anymore.

Actually, "friend" is probably a little generous. He's always been that cocky, good ol' boy type, but he was much more tolerable when we were teenagers. He's a whole adult these days, with a blue-collar job and a wife and kids. No time for fun shit like this anymore. At least, that's what he tells anyone who will listen to him bitch. Yet here he is.

"Hey, man," I greet him, plastering a polite smile on my face and waving. "How have you been?" He takes a swig from a bottle of what I assume is the cheapest beer they sell here. I glance at the sign on the wall behind him stating "No Alcohol Outside of Dining Area" and back, but his unobservant ass doesn't notice. Not that I expect him to.

"Oh, I'm great," he shouts over the noise. "Had a night off from the family so I hit up Jay and we came out here. He's around here somewhere."

I nod knowingly, as if I have any fucking clue what it's like to need a "night off from the family". He claps me on the shoulder like he's a wise older man and not someone I once paid a nickel to eat a rock. His eyes dart behind me to Callie and I can already see his wheels turning so I grab her hand and tug her to my side.

"This is my," I start, and realize I don't want to call her my 'friend' because that's not generous enough, but I don't want to call her something more and freak her out. His lecherous gaze drifts down her body and back up, not quite making it to her face before he stalls. "Uh, this is Callie."

He's still staring at her chest and I'm thirty seconds from punching him in the throat.

"She just moved here. I'm showing her around town. Callie, this is Brendan. We went to school together." His eyes finally make their way back up to her face.

Callie's lips curl up and she sticks a hand out for him to shake, seemingly oblivious to his perving. The look on his face when he grabs her hand is borderline feral, and he starts to pull her to him.

"Well, it's an absolute pleasure to meet you, Miss Callie," he coos, the words dripping from his mouth like sludge. I'm definitely about to hit him. He pulls her hand a little harder, trying to bring it to his mouth to kiss it, and she stumbles forward. Before I can step in and probably end up getting arrested, she yanks her hand from his grip and slaps a saccharine smile on her face.

"It's lovely to meet you, Brendan. Next time, maybe I can meet your wife." She eyes the hand he didn't just have her in a vice grip with, and the plain gold band on his ring finger.

At least he has the decency to look embarrassed. He jams his left hand in his pocket like being married was the only issue.

Callie takes a step back and tucks herself under my arm, sliding her hand across my back and looking up at me. I'm not sure if she's just trying to get Brendan to leave her alone, but I'm definitely not complaining.

"Food time?" I think she only mouthed the words, but Brendan unfortunately either heard, lip-read, or guessed what she said because now he's nodding his head and accepting an invitation that wasn't even for him.

"I'll go get Jay and meet you guys at a table!" He disappears into the crowd.

"Sorry," I grimace. I'm waiting for her to pull away from me now that he's gone but she's still stuck like glue, and it feels like every part of me that's touching her is on fire. "He's kind of a giant douchebag. He wasn't that bad when we were kids."

"It's okay, I've dealt with much worse," she laughs. I'm about to ask for a detailed list of who could possibly be worse, for science of course, but then she squeezes the hand that she's got wrapped around my waist and I forget what I was mad about. "Glad I had you around, though." She pulls away from me and I'm immediately disappointed, but then she snags my hand and laces her fingers in mine. I can feel the heat rush to my cheeks, and I know she sees it because she flashes a triumphant grin at me, her vengeance for her earlier embarrassment finally attained.

What a great fucking night.

Chapter Seven

Callie leads me back to the lobby and through the door to the restaurant, my hand still firmly clasped in hers. We break apart long enough to hit the bathrooms and wash off all the arcade germs. I drop into a booth, and she scoots in next to me.

"Thanks for that," she hums. "I had a great time. I'm starving now, though. What's good to eat here?" She reaches over me to slide a menu out from the stand on the table and lays it out in front of us. "Oh, this looks good!" She points to a picture of a giant plate of nachos and then looks at me expectantly, but she's so close to me right now that my brain is short circuiting. I'm not even sure what she's asking but it doesn't really matter so I just smile and nod. I could have just agreed to give her a kidney, and I'd be fine with it.

A waiter comes over to take our order, and she takes the reins, greeting him with way more sunshine than he's used to. She orders a big platter of supreme nachos, a sweet tea for herself, and manages to coax a preference of root beer out of me. I realize she was asking if I wanted to get this gigantic plate of nachos to share with her, and I'm glad I managed to respond because fuck yes, I do.

As the waiter turns to leave, she gently lays a hand on my knee and leans into my shoulder. Somewhere in my little lizard brain, an instinct tells me to wrap my arm around her shoulder, so I do. Her contented sigh tells me it was the right thing to do, and for the first time, I think I might actually pull off a successful date.

Then, of course, the Dickhead Brigade enters the chat.

Brendan and Jay come bounding through the door, beer sloshing out of the bottles in their hands as they shove each other around and make asses of themselves. They're shouting at each other, and people in the restaurant are turning to glare now. I genuinely couldn't imagine being that embarrassing in public.

Then they spot us and start whooping, and I cringe when I realize it's because my arm is around Callie. I'm trying to remember how many years you get for manslaughter when they rush our table and slide in the booth, shaking the table with their general buffoonery.

I look at her in silent question. *Should I move my arm?* She squeezes my knee with a small smile and thank fuck because I've already considered soldering it to her. I sigh. *Time to get this over with.*

"Callie, you already met Brendan, and this is Jay. Jay, Callie." I point to the poof of long curly hair surrounding the vague shape of a human being. He's got a red flannel tied around his waist over a black Metallica t-shirt that's more hole than shirt at this point, and he's sliding a beanie back over his mess of hair after swiping it back from Brendan's pocket. That must be what they were yelling about when they walked in. I shoot them both warning looks.

Brendan holds up both hands in surrender, and Jay is significantly less of a pig than he is, so I relax a little. Callie starts rubbing little circles on my kneecap with her thumb and my soul leaves my body for a second. She really is trying to kill me.

"It's nice to meet you!" She beams, but she learned her lesson about handshakes and her hands are currently preoccupied with driving me insane, so they stick to verbal pleasantries only.

"It's been a while. How have you been, dude?" I'm pretty sure Jay watched Dazed and Confused at one point in his childhood and just adopted it as his personality for life. I actually kind of like him, to be honest. He just has questionable taste in friends.

"I'm good. Working security at the Panacea Center. What about you?"

"Oh man, I got this new machining job at that factory in town, and they pay like forty bucks an hour. It's boring as fuck but it's easy money. My girl moved in with me, too. So now my apartment's got all kinds of girly shit in it, but it's clean now and it always smells nice so it's all good."

Callie lets out a soft giggle and I'm positive I can feel it in my bones. Jay's a nice guy, and he's good with tech, but otherwise I'm pretty sure he's got maybe three brain cells hiding in that beanie. Callie seems to like him too, and I feel a little better about them crashing our date.

This *is* a date, right? As if on cue, she squeezes my knee again and I swear she can read my mind. The contact brings me back to the conversation.

"That's awesome, man. I'm happy for you."

"Thanks, dude. Shauna's great, too. She's got me doing all kinds of healthy shit. She got me new clothes for work and everything. She made me..." He pauses before backtracking, quieter now. "I, uh... I didn't have time for the band anymore, so I quit. We still play in Johnny's garage sometimes, though." I can tell there's definitely more to that story, but I'm not going to push it tonight. "What about you? What have you been up to outside of work?"

It's a simple question, but now I'm debating whether I want to mention my book idea to them. I wanted to tell Callie all about it tonight, but I'm not sure if I want it to be a group project. *Fuck it*, I decide. I'll give them the bare minimum and talk to her about it after they leave.

"Well, I actually came up with an idea for a book I want to write. It's not much yet, but I've been working on that, mostly." My gaze drifts to Callie. She rolls her lips into a flat line and looks at the floor. I regret this decision immediately, but I don't know why.

"Dude, that's so cool! Is it like a fantasy story or what?" I nod, and I know I've lost what little of Brendan's attention I had. The only fantasy he's interested in is fantasy football. He's scrolling through his phone now. Maybe if I downplay it, we can move on?

"Yeah, I came up with the idea at work and it all just flowed out into an outline before I knew it. I don't know if it'll even go anywhere. It's not that great yet, just a vague idea." Callie pulls her hand away and starts picking at her nails and my stomach plummets. I'm not sure what exactly I said wrong, but I can tell she's uncomfortable now. I give her shoulder a light squeeze and she looks up at me with a weak smile. I've got to turn this around or the ship is going to sink before it ever sets sail.

I'm spared the hassle of coming up with a reason to kick them from the party when Jay's phone starts vibrating on the table.

"Ah, shit," he mutters, swiping the phone from the table. "That's my girl. She must be coming home early. Time to go, B." We exchange parting pleasantries, but the relief is short-lived. Callie's still picking at her nails when the waiter stops at our table and deposits a plate of nachos the size of a hubcap in front of us. "Enjoy," he mumbles, clearly hating every second of his job. He slides a handful of wet wipe packets under the edge of the plate and then he's gone. I take my arm back and grab a stack of napkins from the dispenser.

"This looks so good, but it's about to get messy," I say, tapping her hand to get her attention. She snaps out of it a bit and agrees, picking out a nacho piled high with chicken and cheese and carefully taking a bite. I decide maybe the direct route is best with her. I've noticed that she's definitely got people-pleasing tendencies, and I don't think she's actually going to tell me what's wrong unless I ask.

"Hey, is everything okay? Sorry about the guys, it's hard to go anywhere in a town this small without running into someone you know."

"Oh, it's fine! I just get quiet around new people sometimes," she explains, but it still sounds like she's holding something back. "So, tell me more about this book." She shovels another nacho into her mouth and waits.

It's go time.

"Ok, so basically it's a classic D&D campaign-style fantasy. There's a party of adventurers and they come up to this little village in the mountains and the innkeeper tells them that they'll need to lock themselves in their rooms at night because there's a monster roaming the village after dark and no one can quite pin down what the monster is but they know it's taking people from their beds in the night and they're never seen again. There are no bodies, no blood, no traces of a struggle, nothing. They're just gone."

In the midst of my infodump, it seems like whatever was bothering her has faded. She's got her head resting on her hand while she listens intently, nachos temporarily forgotten, so I continue.

"The party agrees to investigate and kill the monster in exchange for food and lodging while they're in the village.

They spend a few nights staked out and find that the monster is actually a woman, and she's not taking anyone. She's helping women and children escape from the village because a band of bandits has taken over the town and enlisted all the men to join them. It's no longer safe for those who can't defend themselves, so the woman, whose husband was murdered by the bandits because he wouldn't join them, is helping them escape into the next town over and she has plans to fake their deaths once she gets everyone out."

She still looks interested. Good, I'm not boring her yet. I feel like I'm word-vomiting and I'm not great at explaining things out loud, so I rush through the ending.

"So, the party agrees to help her take out the bandits instead. I'm still working on the fine details but I'm thinking the leader of the party is going to be a woman who took up adventuring after she killed her abusive husband and went on the run, so she's going to be extra willing to help. Maybe when they're done, they invite the woman to join their party."

She's quiet for a moment, and I'm about to open my mouth to tell her I know it's not that great, and it's okay if she doesn't think it sounds interesting and whatever other self-deprecating bullshit I can say to make her not feel bad for hating it when a smile splits her face.

"Holy shit, Devon. That sounds amazing."

My jaw drops. "You think?"

"Yes! I'd read the shit out of that!"

Now it's my turn to glow, and she leans back into my shoulder, so I slip my arm around her again. It's always felt awkward sitting like this with anyone else, but she fits tucked under my arm perfectly. It's like I was made to be wrapped around her. We both eat in easy silence for a few minutes before she turns enough to look up at me again.

"So, where'd you get the idea?"

Do I tell her the truth about the annotations and risk her

thinking I'm nuts? Or do I lie? I don't think I could lie to her even if I wanted to, and I'm honestly not surprised to find that I really *don't* want to, so here goes nothing.

"Well," I start, dragging out the word. "You know that book you set aside for me the other day?"

"Yeah," she nods, and now she's smiling. She has to know about it already, because the look on her face is purely conspiratorial. She must realize it, too, because she quickly shifts into an innocent smile.

"When I started reading it, I noticed that there was a bunch of handwriting in the margins." I pause, giving her the opportunity to say something about it before I dive headfirst into it, but she just crinkles her eyebrows at me.

"There wasn't anything written in it when I took it off the shelf," she says mildly, but I can tell she's full of shit. "Unless I missed it?"

"No, you definitely would have seen it. It's on almost every page. It's okay, though. I didn't think much of it because it was a used book, but then I started reading the notes and they were actually really insightful. I spent the whole night reading the book, and it was pretty good, but it was the annotations that gave me the idea."

I thought that would be the embarrassing part, but she nods like this all makes perfect sense to her. The anxiety over the last part is what's really going to give me a heart attack, though.

"Well, and... uh... and you kind of inspired it, too." Her eyes widen, and I rush to explain, looking down at the table before I lose my nerve. "The woman in the village, the one that's saving all the people? I don't know, I just kind of imagined her with your face. And things are rough for her now, but before the villains showed up, she was a lot like you. All sunshine and kindness. She's not all fleshed out yet, but I think she's going to have a flower and herb shop where she sold arrangements and remedies before everything went down. So, when they kill her husband and destroy her shop, they think they kill her too, but she uses her healing knowledge and survives."

She lays a hand over mine on the table, and I glance back at her. "She didn't need to be strong before," she muses. "So, she didn't know she could."

"Yeah," I whisper, because of course she understands perfectly. "And I don't know, I know I don't know a ton about your life yet or anything, but it just reminded me of you. You seem like the type of person who's stronger than you know."

She looks up at me, pulling away just enough to put a few inches between us, and her eyes are watery. Fuck, did I say something wrong again? But then the corners of her mouth curl up, and before I even realize what's happening, her hands are locked together behind my neck and she's closing the distance.

Oh, thank fuck.

Chapter Eight

Obviously, I had high hopes that this is how this evening would end up going, but I definitely didn't expect her to start it. I figured I'd make a snap decision and go for it, and maybe she'd kiss me back to be polite, or maybe she'd punch me in the face and call an Uber. But here she is, arms wrapped around my neck, soft lips on mine, and I'm completely frozen.

I realize with horror that I'm still buffering and not actually reciprocating, and I need to change that immediately. Retroactively, if possible. I glide a hand up the line of her jaw, tilting her face and deepening the kiss as much as I can while we're both still seated in the booth. Her tongue presses at the seam of my lips and I can feel my blood rushing in my ears. I open, and we become a tangle of tongues and teeth for less than 15 seconds before the trance is broken by someone whistling from across the restaurant.

"Get a room," a teenage boy calls out, presumably the source of the whistle as well, and his gaggle of friends start cackling. I'm categorizing murder charges by the years again when Callie pulls away, lips swollen and face flushed. She looks around to see what caught my attention and her cheeks heat when she sees the table full of boys staring at us and laughing.

I expect her to be embarrassed, but she just laughs back. She lays that hand back on my knee again, a little higher this time, and actually *winks* at me as my leg stiffens under her grip. Among other things. Potentially visible things. *Fuck*. I try to discreetly adjust, but of course she notices.

She lets out a soft chuckle and leans back in the booth, hand still firmly - maybe firmer - in place, and shoves a nacho into her mouth. My eyes are cemented to her lips already, and it takes all of my willpower to drag them back up to her eyes. She is absolutely enjoying herself right now.

"Hmm," she starts, and I can tell by the glint in her eye that she's about to torture the absolute shit out of me. She sticks another nacho in her mouth and examines her fingers while she chews. Then, in what could be deemed as an act of war, she looks down at the wet wipe packs and then stares me right in the eye and sucks her thumb into her mouth. She hollows out her cheeks and sucks off whatever probably imaginary residue was on it. Yep, incoming cardiac arrest. She's an actual serial killer.

I try to groan quietly, but it comes out as a growl. The look on her face shifts from mischievous to downright feral and I'm immediately trying to memorize the noise I made so I can do it again later. She releases her thumb with a tiny pop and pushes down on my thigh to lift herself up in her seat, brushing the top of her nose along my jawline.

"I think I've had enough of the arcade," she mumbles, her breath heating the shell of my ear. Her lips graze my cheek as she sinks back down beside me, and I fight to suppress the next groan because I know it will *not* be quiet. I quickly rip open a wet wipe and clean up, tossing it on top of the half-eaten nachos.

I manage a grunt of agreement, and she scoots out of the

booth. I stand up and immediately regret that decision, along with the decision to wear a particularly tight pair of jeans today. Luckily, Callie is standing directly in front of me, so my bulge is concealed from the general public. I slip some cash from my wallet and leave it on the table with the bill.

When I turn back to her, she's looking back at me over her shoulder with a wicked grin, and my brain ceases all rational thought. I slither one hand around her waist, settling low on her hip, and bury my face in her hair. With a memorizing inhale, I tilt my body around her so she can see my lips.

"Definitely time to go," I whisper, my right hand squeezing her hip and pulling her back into me. She arches her back just enough to rub her ass against the hard ridge already threatening to tear a seam in my jeans and I wince at the involuntary groan I let out. People are starting to look at us again.

"You're fucking trouble, you know that?" I mumble to myself, but I already know that she's well and truly fucking aware. It takes every ounce of willpower I have but I give her hip a gentle push towards the door.

She stays close, aware that she's the only thing blocking the view. As soon as we're outside, I shift so I'm walking next to her, but my hand doesn't leave her hip until we're coming up on the passenger side of my car. I use my grip to spin her around and clamp my hand down on the roof of the car next to her head, my other hand sliding up to the side of her throat. My fingers splay across her cheek, and I use my thumb to tilt her head back. She meets my eyes and her gaze is molten.

I'm still waiting to snap out of it and wake up in bed with a hard on.

She surges up on her toes and her mouth is on mine again. My thumb slides down, my hand wrapping around the column of her throat, and I squeeze softly without thinking. *Fuck*. I'm not sure what's possessing me, but I've never acted like this before. Never *needed* like this before.

I release my hand and pull away, an apology ready, but the moan she lets out and the look of desperate need on her face has my hand right back where it was. Her gaze flicks back and forth between my eyes for a moment before it drifts behind me, scanning the parking lot full of cars.

Her eyebrows knit together, and I can see her wheels turning. The lampposts are far enough apart that there's not much light on us, but there's enough. Anyone walking past could see us. Her expression is torn between want and fear. I run my thumb over her pulse point gently, comfortingly. A promise without words. *It's your choice.* Her decision flashes across her face, heated and heady, as if there was never another choice to begin with.

"So..." she rasps, placing her hand gently over the one I've got wrapped around her throat and holding it in place. "Where to next?" She digs two fingers into the waistband of my jeans and yanks me forward. I brace the arm on the car just in time to avoid crushing her. *Okay, that's it.*

I grab her chin in the palm of my hand, a little rougher than I intended to, and lean in close. "Fucking troublemaker," I grit out. She should definitely be pulling away at this point, but her impish smile and heated eyes tell me that she's exactly where she wants to be. The point is further proven when she snakes one hand up to the back of my neck, nails digging into skin, and uses the other to palm my cock through my jeans.

"Then *fuck* the *troublemaker*, Devon."

I take a deep breath as the last thread of my self-control snaps. I spin her by her hips and pin her against the side of the car, burying my face in the crook of her shoulder again. She smells like lavender and something woody, like cedar or sandalwood. I take another deep breath, embedding it into my brain. I roll my hips against her, digging into her ass, and she lets out a breathy moan. My right hand comes up to wrap lightly around her throat again while the other holds her in place, still wrapped around her hip.

She tilts her head back a bit, and it feels like an invitation, so I squeeze just a little tighter. The strangled moan she lets out tells me that was exactly what she was asking for, so I press in on the sides a bit more, not enough to cut off her breath yet, and slide my other hand up her side. Her skin feels like it's on fire through the fabric of her sweater, and I need to feel it on my own skin immediately. I skate my hand back down to her waist and up under her sweater, trailing my fingertips up her ribs in gentle strokes. Callie gasps, arching her back at my touch, so I flatten my palm against her and pull her back against my chest.

"Fucking *perfect*," I rumble against her ear. I'm close enough that she can probably hear me, but she definitely felt it with her back pressed tightly against my chest. My hand grazes up farther, slipping under the wire of her bra to palm her breast as she moans again. They're the perfect size for a handful, like I was meant to be holding them at all times. Maybe I can convince her. Probably not. We'll see.

My fingers brush over her hardened nipple and her hand flies up to my forearm, nails digging into my skin. The sting from the punctures makes me flex my hand on her throat, eliciting the sweetest whimper I've ever heard. I roll her nipple between my fingers and it's a good thing I've got her pinned to the car because her knees buckle. She digs her nails deeper into my arm. "Please," she begs, pushing back against me as hard as she can.

Well, how could I deny her when she asks so nicely?

I gently trail my fingers back down her side, slow enough to be torture, and take half a step back. Before she can protest my absence, I slide my hand inside her leggings and run my middle finger up her dripping center. *Fuck, literally dripping.* I repeat the motion, pressing a little further in every time. She tries to grind down, but I'm not done tormenting just yet, so I hold her in place with the hand under her chin.

My chest rumbles with a warning growl and she tilts her head back, leaning it against my shoulder. Her lips are parted, breath coming out in quick, faint pants, and I realize that the hand around her throat is almost fully constricting her air. I release most of the pressure, but she uses the newfound freedom to whip her head as far in my direction as she can and glare daggers at me. *Okay, then. Good to know.*

I squeeze again, a little tighter than before, and she lays her head back again. The fingers she has wrapped around my forearm hook deeper in, the nails definitely breaking skin, like she's trying to hold me in place. *Don't worry, troublemaker. I'm not going anywhere.*

Based on the slickness coating my hand, I decide she's waited long enough. I plunge two fingers inside her, twisting so my thumb presses on her clit, and the gasp she lets out could burn me alive. I slowly work my fingers in and out, filling her as far as I can and stroking her walls on the way out. I move my thumb in small circles in time with the fingers she's currently strangling and her hand flies up to cover her mouth just in time to mask a muffled scream.

She swivels her head, frantically looking for anyone who might have heard her, but I genuinely couldn't give a fuck less if someone hears us. Or sees us. I feel like I should, because no one else deserves to experience her like this. Fuck, I don't even deserve it, but we'll revisit that when I'm not currently three knuckles deep in her.

Faint laughter rings out from across the parking lot, followed by the music and chirps of arcade games. Callie freezes, her gaze shooting to the entrance with wide eyes. "Shit," she mouths, eyes locked around my shoulder on whoever just came out. I pause, ready to stop if she asks, but she clamps down on my fingers as her eyes slowly drift from the interlopers back to me. She nods, urging me on, and goes back to watching over my shoulder. I'm not sure if she's afraid they'll catch us or hoping they do, but a car door closes in the distance, and her eyes are back on mine and full of heat.

She tenses, arching her back and pressing into my hand. I release the pressure on the sides of her throat and move my hand up to cup her chin, tilting her face away from mine and trailing light kisses up the side of her exposed neck and jaw. As soon as the blood starts to rush back to her head, she tenses again, falling apart against me and biting down another moan. I thrust both fingers as far into her as I can and hold them there, rubbing slow circles with my thumb while she rides out the orgasm.

Overly sensitive, she twitches with my movements and grabs at my wrist. I withdraw, placing a kiss on her temple. She goes entirely limp against me, so I release her jaw and gently turn her back to face me. Her hands slide up to my face and her eyes are lust-drunk and hooded as she stares up at me, a sated smile forming as she comes back down to reality. But I'm not quite done tormenting her, and I'm definitely not sated yet.

She reaches for my belt, but I stop her with one hand, meeting her gaze as I bring the other hand - the one covered in her - to my mouth. Her gaze turns molten, and neither of us blinks as I suck them clean. Her mouth parts for a moment and then she's pulling me down to her by my collar with intent to devour. Our tongues clash, and I'm sure I taste like her, but that seems just fine with her by the small moans I'm muffling with my own.

She tries to reach for me again and I stop with a hand around her wrist. I pull back and rest my forehead on hers so I can process rational thought for a second before speaking. I lean back just far enough so she can see my lips because I don't want to be farther than her than I absolutely have to be.

"Unless you want the whole state to know what we're up to right now, we're gonna need to pause the game here." I smooth her hair down and plant a kiss on her forehead. "To be continued."

"To be continued," she repeats with an absolutely feral grin, her gaze dipping down to my painfully hard cock before opening her door and ducking into the car. "Let's get going, then. It's a long, *hard* drive home," she tosses over her shoulder with a look of pure mischief aimed directly at the *hard* part of the drive.

Oh, I am so fucked.

Chapter Nine

The drive back to town is spent with my hand on Callie's thigh. She laces her fingers through mine and thank fuck I don't need to shift because I don't think I could bring myself to pull my hand away. She leans sideways in her seat so she can see my face, her free hand propped on her elbow and fisted under her chin. The first few minutes of the drive are quiet. I feel like I should be panicking about that, but it's a peaceful quiet. Not an "I regret that" quiet.

Every time I glance over at her, her smile gets a little bigger. I give her thigh a light squeeze and turn towards her.

"So," I start, dragging the last letter out a little longer than necessary. I'm definitely procrastinating. She tilts her head, waiting for whatever dumb shit is about to fall out of my mouth and surprise us both. Suddenly my mouth is drier than the fucking Sahara. I clear my throat and try again. "It's not too late. Is there... uh... anywhere else you want to go tonight?" I immediately wince because *are you fucking kidding me? That's the best I could come up with?* Whatever, it's too late now.

Please say my house please say my house please say my house please say

"Well, I'm off tomorrow too, so I don't have to be up early," she muses, unfurling a finger from her fist and tapping it to her lips. "Oh, I know! We could do the Seven Wonders!"

Not what I had in mind, but definitely better than calling it a night. I can work with that.

"Well, the park closes at dark, so that knocks out the trail, the gazebo and the dog park. We already ate, so we can save the Mexican restaurant for next time." I realize too late how presumptuous that last part was. I steal a quick glance at her to gauge her reaction, but there is none. Just her eager smile.

She mentioned earlier that she wanted *us* to go see the cows, so I guess it wasn't as presumptuous as my anxiety is telling me it was. Not to mention the fact that I was inside her ten minutes ago. But she spent an entire evening with me and she's still anticipating a next time. Something in my chest squeezes tight. *Haven't fucked it up yet, lover boy.*

"You've obviously already been to the bookstore," I continue, but she interrupts me.

"The cows!" She's practically vibrating with excitement, and I can't help but laugh.

"The cows unfortunately have a bedtime, unless you want to add a B&E to your record," I explain. She sticks that bottom lip out again in a pout and my brain ever so kindly graces me with a mental image of her wrapping those lips around–

SPRAY BOTTLE. NOW.

I manage to downgrade the ensuing groan to a heavy sigh. I adjust my jeans as discreetly as possible but *of course* she clocks the motion again. Her eyes shoot back to mine and her pout morphs into a smirk, one eyebrow arching. *Damn it.*

She slowly unlaces her fingers from mine and glides them up my forearm. I stop her with a look, and she halts, her eyebrows scrunching together in confusion. Shit, this is the second time I've stopped her. She thinks I'm rejecting her.

"Callie, listen," I say with a sigh. "If you so much as look in my direction like that right now, I have absolutely zero faith in my ability not to wreck this car and kill us both," I blurt out, sliding my hand under hers and lacing our fingers back together. I lift our hands up and press a kiss to her knuckles before laying my palm back on her thigh. I've decided it lives there permanently now. I'll file the change of address tomorrow.

"Oh," she exhales, pink creeping up her cheeks again. I'm starting to worry about her blood flow at this point.

"Yeah, *oh*. Troublemaker," I tell her with a smirk, and she gives my fingers a squeeze. "Anyway, that leaves us with one option."

Her eyes widen as she realizes where we're going. "But, how? I thought you had to check with your cousin first?" I toss her a look of mock offense.

"Please. If you think for one second that I didn't text him as soon as we got to the arcade, then you're thoroughly underestimating me." She lets out a little squeal and leans forward, planting a kiss on my cheek.

I think I'm starting to worry about my own blood flow, too.

We pull up to the bowling alley and the lights are off. I park in the back of the building and use the door code my cousin gave me, holding the door open for her to step inside. I walk ahead of her, leading the way to the electric panel that turns the whole place on. Callie eyes the darkness warily, but I've always had great night vision. I consider being a gentleman and taking her hand to lead her until I get to the light switches, but where's the fun in that?

She doesn't notice as I slow down and let her walk past me. She doesn't notice when I creep up behind her and crouch down to her height. She does, however, notice when I wrap one arm around her waist from behind and lift her in the air.

The growl I let loose is entirely self-serving, but I'd bet she can feel it rumble against her back.

She opens her mouth to scream just as I clamp my hand over it. Her eyes must finally be adjusting, because she jerks in my arms as she realizes she's face to face with someone. It takes her a second to realize that someone is herself, one of my arms banded around her waist and the other wrapped around her face. We lock eyes over her shoulder in the wall of mirrors in front of us and she relaxes as soon as she sees the sly look on my face.

I set her back down on her feet, and the hand over her mouth slides down to her chin. She tilts her head back and I lean forward to capture her lips again. She grinds her ass against me and I groan, my hand instantly tightening on her chin. I break the kiss and push my chest against her back, walking us a few steps forward until we're almost touching the mirror. She meets my eyes again in the mirror just as I press my knee between hers and kick one of her legs out.

Callie lets out a soft gasp as she loses her balance. Both hands fly out in front of her and her palms slap against the mirror above her head. I press against her back, pushing her flush against the mirror, and drag my hands down to her hips. Her breath is heavy, fogging up the glass before us. My hands slip under the hem of her sweater and roam over her bare skin before dipping under the waistband of her leggings. She leans her head back against my chest and her eyes flutter closed.

My hands return to her hips, and I pull her against me, digging the hard ridge of my cock against the small of her back. I brush her hair to the side and gently ghost my lips over the tiny tattoos trailing down her spine. They're all symbols that I don't recognize, surrounded by a bar on either side made up of a geometric pattern. She releases a breathy moan as one of her hands slides up my thigh. She finds my gaze in the mirror and quirks an eyebrow in question.

"Fuck, yes please," I grind out with a nod, and she's immediately palming my cock through my jeans. I try to suppress my groan, but then she's squeezing and it's all I can do not to fucking whimper, so self-control is obviously on hold for the evening. Honestly, whatever. We've got the place to ourselves anyway.

Before I know what's happening, she's already spinning around to face me. She looks up at me through her lashes, her smirk dripping sin, and she pushes me back a step with one finger. Both palms flatten against my chest and slither down. She doesn't break eye contact as she drops to her knees, and the involuntary whimper I let out is almost embarrassing. *Almost.*

She keeps her eyes on me as she undoes my belt. When she pops the button on my jeans, her tongue darts out over her bottom lip and I swear my eyes roll back in my head. Suddenly her hands aren't on me anymore and my gaze shoots back to her just in time to see her peeling her sweater over her head. Another tattoo pokes up from below her waistband, curling around the ball of her hip. Snakes, maybe? She slips it under her knees, cushioning them from the waxed wood floor, and bright blue eyes bore into me again as she yanks my jeans down enough to pull my cock out of them.

Callie's hands are warm as she wraps them both around my base. I brace myself against the mirror with one hand and the other drifts to the back of her head as she wraps her lips around my tip. She swirls her tongue along the underside of my cock and I'm already seeing fucking stars. She bobs her head back and forth a few inches and then hollows out her cheeks and sucks. My brain might actually be short circuiting, and sparks shoot up my spine with every drag of her tongue.

There's no way in hell I'm going to last any respectable amount of time if she keeps this up.

I tip my head back, breaking our eye contact and trying to concentrate on literally anything else, but sharp nails bite into the back of my thigh, and I whip my gaze back down to her. She's glaring at me through watery eyes, mouth stretched around me, and the message is clear. *She wants me to watch.* I nod and run my fingers through her hair, pulling the stray strands out of her face. I can either look her in the eyes as she swallows me whole, or I can watch us both in the mirror, and I'm not even sure which option is less hot. *Fuck.*

I opt to watch her directly, and oh *fuck* was that the right choice. She moans around my cock and the vibration from it shoots directly to my spine. She removes one hand from me and sucks me straight down her throat, completely bottoming out, and I'm immediately seeing stars.

The hand she removed from me is now expertly unclasping her bra in the back. She discards it on the ground next to us and her hand drifts up to cup a breast and squeeze. I think I'd sell an organ in exchange for an arm long enough to reach the other one, but it's just out of reach. She's still bobbing back and forth, my hand resting gently on her head, as she takes her nipple between her fingers and rolls it, gracing me with a rumbling moan again. My eyes zero in on every movement, taking note for later.

Hyperfocusing on her hand awards me a small amount of control, but then she throws that out the window too when that hand drifts south. She runs her fingertips gently along her waistband before diving her hand in and I involuntarily fist the back of her hair. Before I can loosen my grip, her eyes turn pleading, and she gives me an encouraging moan. *Use me.*

Fuck. I drop my half-assed grip on her hair and try again, sliding my fingers up the nape of her neck and curling as much of her short hair between my fingers as I can. She continues working herself as I push harder on the back of her head, keeping the same pace but pressing deeper into her throat. Tears leak from the corners of her eyes and her lips thin as they stretch to accommodate me. The sight of her alone is enough to make the tension at the base of my spine bubble over.

The hand she has wrapped around my base squeezes tighter and my already flimsy focus snaps like a rubber band. As phenomenal as her mouth feels, I need to be inside her immediately. I can't explain it, but the need is all-consuming. I use my grip on her hair to pull her back and my cock falls out of her mouth with a pop. Her eyebrows pinch in confusion, until I'm hauling her up by her shoulder. Her hair still fisted in one hand, I slip the other around the column of her throat and feel her swallow and she gazes up at me with heavy-lidded eyes. I gently yank her hair back, angling her face up and leaning in for a punishing kiss.

I slowly walk her backwards into the mirror and pull back from the kiss just before her ass hits the glass. She glares at me, panting, and I arch an eyebrow at her.

"Well, aren't you a needy thing," I mutter, releasing my hold on her to drag both hands down her bare sides and settle on her hips. She returns the sentiment by grabbing a handful of balls and squeezing. I exhale a groan, and I catch my eyes darkening in the mirror behind her. The flash of fear on her face tells me she sees it too. It only lasts a second before her gaze heats.

That's it, she's fucked around enough. Time to find out.

I spin her around by her hips until she's facing the mirror again and cage her in with one hand planted against the glass on either side of her head. She catches my eye in the mirror and every square inch of my skin heats at her smirk. Fog forms on the mirror around my hands, with another little puff of fog between them from her panting breath.

I'll be back here tomorrow morning cleaning handprints and scrubbing this place down for hours. *Worth it.*

I slip one finger into the back of her waistband and let it snap back, our eyes still locked in the mirror. "Off," I growl. She wastes no time, hooking her thumbs in to slip them down her legs and tossing them on the pile with her sweater. My lips part and every muscle in my body freezes as I take her in. Her shoulders are narrow, her waist tapering in just a bit before flaring out into wide hips wrapped in nothing but black lace. I run my fingers along the tiny white lines and dimples covering the surface of them and she shivers.

I slip my hands back around her waist and trace the edges of the lace. Not quite a thong, but dangerously close. I don't miss the fact that it matches the bra on the discard pile perfectly. I may not have anticipated this, but she did. *Fuck, that makes this whole thing so much hotter.* The urge to rip the flimsy lace straight off of her body is overwhelming, but I settle for sliding them down myself. I let out an involuntary groan as they fall and she kicks them into the pile too.

With her legs now bare, I can see the rest of the tattoo on her thigh in the mirror. The curling bits at the top are the snakes making up the top of a Medusa head. It's part of a larger collage of what looks like scenes from Greek mythology. I realize that's what the bars on the sides of her spine look like. I read somewhere that they're called Greek *meandros*, like the borders on fabrics and paintings.

This is so not the most important thing to be thinking about right now, you fucking nerd. Right. Anyway.

Her gaze meets mine in the mirror and her cheeks heat when she sees me staring. Probably drooling. *Shit.* Her eyes narrow and she stares pointedly at my chest. "Off," she commands, and I don't hesitate to oblige. I toss the button up off, slip my t-shirt over my head, and kick off my jeans. The second I'm upright again, she backs up into me, leaning forward with her palms pressed on the glass.

I groan and widen my stance to meet her height, leaning forward to mold my body against her back. I dig my fingertips into her hips and pull her back, my still painfully hard cock sliding between the apex of her thighs like it was meant to be there. My right hand skates over her hip and across her burning center while the left holds her firmly in place. I dip my middle finger through her wetness, dragging it up to her clit as her breath catches. I mimic the small circles she used on herself earlier and her silence quickly becomes gasping moans. Her head leans back, eyes shooting open to meet mine in the reflection.

That's right, troublemaker. I took notes.

I slip two thick fingers inside and continue the circles with my thumb, her whole body tensing. She bucks back against me, and the friction is almost enough to do me in early. As if she knows I'm already tiptoeing on the edge, she turns to look at me. "Please," she pleads in between pants, her hand reaching behind her to grab my cock. *Oh, she's definitely trying to kill me.*

I pause, quickly realizing that I wasn't anticipating this, so *I did not come prepared.* Of course she notices the look of sheer panic on my face, because she fucking notices everything. And then she *laughs* and I'm about to spiral when she lays a hand over the one I'm currently digging into her hip.

"S'ok," she mumbles. "Covered and clean." *Oh, thank fuck.* Relief washes over me, and I loosen my grip. I get one good exhale out before my brain fully processes what she's telling me, and I let out a feral growl. Didn't expect to be that excited about it but here we are. *New kink unlocked, I guess?*

With thoroughly renewed vigor, I press her hip back against me again, harder than before. My hand tangles into the back of her hair, pushing her face down and bending her over farther. Her palms squeak against the glass as she slides them down with her and we both stop for a second to laugh. Her eyes are still locked on me in the mirror when I position the head of my cock at her entrance. Her jaw drops open on a moan as I press in slowly, stretching her walls around me.

Once I'm fully inside, I give her a second to adjust, releasing my grip on her hair and instead wrapping my fingers around the nape of her neck. Her muscles tighten around me as I pull almost all the way out before slamming back inside. Her strangled scream echoes through the bowling alley and I continue thrusting at a punishing pace. She mumbles between moans, an unintelligible combination of "fuck" and something that might be another language.

I can feel the heat trickling down my spine, but I need to get one more out of her before I'm done. The hand on the back of her neck snakes around and molds around her throat, pulling her head back against me and stepping forward to press her skin against the cold mirror.

I continue driving into her, the hand around her hip drifting down again to slip through her wetness. I can feel her whole body tensing up and I release her throat, all the blood rushing to her head. Her pussy tightens around me as she falls over the edge with a loud groan and takes me right along with her. I thrust into her as far as I can and hold there, her walls fluttering around my cock as I empty deep inside her with a rasping moan.

A whimper escapes her, and she starts to slide out of my grip. My arm wraps around her waist before she can fall forward, the other arm bracing us against the mirror. If I could live like this, inside her and around her, I would. I turn us around and sag down the mirror to the floor. Mostly because neither of us is capable of conscious thought right now, let alone vertical stability. The mirror is like ice on my back, and it brings me back to consciousness.

Both arms wrap around her middle, holding her tight to me. I swipe the sweat-soaked hair from her forehead back and pepper kisses across her face and down the side of her neck, pausing just below her ear to bury my face in the crook of her shoulder. We sit in comfortable silence like that for a few minutes before she mumbles something about cleaning up and I nod, helping her lift herself off of me.

We both stand, legs wobbling, and she turns to grab her pile of clothes. *Nope, I'm not done yet.* I grab her wrist and spin her back to me, catching her in my arms before she can lose her balance. Both of my hands come down in a gentle smack, a handful of ass cheek in each palm. She beams up at me, slapping a hand against my chest before bouncing up on her toes to crush her lips against mine. Her fingers tangle in my loose hair, the elastic band lost somewhere in the shuffle, and she nips once at my bottom lip.

"Fucking troublemaker," I mumble, and she beams up at me before planting one more kiss. I slip my hands down to the back of her thighs and she squeals as I lift her up and tuck her feet behind me. I walk her over to the couch in the nearest bowling lane and drop her on the cushion.

"Stay," I order. "I'll be back." She waves a hand at me and gives me a noncommittal noise, but she leans back on her elbows and doesn't move. My gaze drags across her flushed skin one more time before I grab my jeans and head to the kitchen.

Chapter Ten

I return a few minutes later with a warm washcloth, some vending machine snacks, and two bottles of water pilfered from the kitchen. Callie hasn't moved, and her eyes are closed. I kneel down on the carpet next to her and bring my hand up the side of her face, turning it toward me and pulling her into a slow kiss. I can feel her smiling against my lips, eyes still closed, and I can't help but return it. I gently tap my finger on her cheek and her eyes drift open to meet mine.

"Snacks and water?" I nod my head toward the tray of junk food on the little table behind me.

"Uh, yes please," she says eagerly, sitting up. I hand her the washcloth to clean up with and go gather her pile of clothes, plopping them down on the couch beside her. She pulls her sweater over her head and slides the thin lace up her legs, curling her feet up under her. I sink into the couch next to her, pulling her into my lap and pressing a kiss to her temple.

We stay there for a while, sharing the snack cache and bullshitting. Her fingers trail over my tattoos, and I explain the references as she waltzes over them. Some she recognizes, like the Balrog whose horns curl around my bicep and the Frankenstein quote shaped into stitches around my shoulder socket. Others she doesn't. Mostly the more modern and non-literary references, like Frostmourne piercing through the Lich King's helmet on my forearm or the lyrics woven throughout the art.

She crunches on some pretzels as I tell her about the progress I made in my book, and I rub little circles on her back with my thumb while she talks about some of the places she's lived. All over the country, plus places like Italy, Greece, and Scotland. This is the first time she's talked about her life before she moved here.

"Italy was my favorite," she tells me. "The food was amazing, and the old buildings are so beautiful. The weather was nice most of the time, too."

"I think I'd like that. Maybe in the winter though. It's super hot in the summer there, isn't it?"

"It is," she agrees. "*So* hot. But it's more dry than humid so it's not that bad."

I wrinkle my nose. "Hot is hot, no matter how dry it is."

"Fair enough," she says, flashing me a grin and tilting her head toward the lane in front of us. "So, did you just bring me here to chit chat all night, or are you ready to get your ass kicked?"

"Oh, that's cute," I tell her with a patronizing glance. "I'll have you know that I grew up in this bowling alley. I'm basically a professional, so I'd be careful how much shit you talk."

Spoiler alert, I am absolutely fucking terrible at bowling.

As soon as I turn around to go turn the lanes on, she beams me in the back of the head with an empty water bottle. "Strike," she calls after me, collapsing in a fit of giggles. *Oh, it's on*.

I head to the back and turn everything on, being careful to leave all the outside lights off. When I return, she's already got a ball picked out from one of the racks for herself. "Shoes?" I ask, and she holds up a bare foot in response. "Alright, but you should know that if you drop that ball and break a toe, I will absolutely laugh at you. Are you sure you don't want gutter guards up?" She flips me off and scoffs.

"Please, this isn't my first rodeo." She turns and waits as the machine finishes setting the pins. "Ladies first," she calls over her shoulder, and runs up to the top of the lane. She rolls the ball down the lane awkwardly and it makes it about halfway before it goes straight into the gutter.

She turns to me with a sheepish smile. "Okay, I may have overexaggerated my experience. I..." She jumps as the ball return clanks and spits her ball out. "I may have possibly never actually been bowling before."

"Ah," I muse, stepping up to her and wrapping my arms around her waist. "So, this *is* your first rodeo?" Her eyes narrow and she glares up at me with faux ferocity. I pull her closer to me and press a kiss to her forehead. "That's okay, I'll let you in on a trade secret. I," I tell her, pointing one finger back at myself. "Am actually an atrocious bowler. The only thing I'm a professional at here is making snacks and talking shit."

She laughs, burying her face in my chest before pulling out of my grip. "Okay, let me try again." She grabs her ball from the return and mimics a line up that I can only assume she's seen in a movie. When she releases the ball, her fingers stick, and she almost goes flying down the lane with it. It takes everything in me not to laugh, but when she turns to me and starts cackling, I join in.

"Alright, I think bowling might not be for me," she concedes.

"Yeah, me neither." I plop back down on the couch. She grabs her ball from the return and puts it back on the shelf before sauntering over to join me. She climbs on my lap, straddling my legs with hers, and curls up against my chest. A yawn escapes her and prompts one of my own.

"I think it's probably time to call it a night," she mumbles against my shoulder. She leans back and stretches her arms over her head.

"Yeah, you're probably right," I agree. "So..." I haven't got the faintest fucking clue how to ask her if she wants me to take her home or if she wants to come to my place without sounding presumptuous. But what if she *wants* me to ask her to come home with me? Luckily, she spares me from the agonizing decision with a hand laid gently on my cheek.

"Hey, you're off work tomorrow, right?" I nod, and her smile spreads. "Got any plans?"

"Not really," I shrug. "I was just going to write for a while. Maybe play some video games." I glance at the mirror wall next to the lane and cringe. "Coming in here before they open and cleaning handprints off the glass," I add.

"Well, don't feel like you have to say yes because I won't be offended, but, if neither of us has anything better to do, maybe I can come home with you? We can get some sleep and some breakfast, and we'll come back here first thing and clean up together and then you can bounce ideas off of me while you write? If you don't want to, it's totally fine, I just-"

I cut off her rambling with the pad of my thumb, slipping my fingers around the back of her neck and pulling her lips to mine.

"Callie," I mumble, pulling back but leaving my fingers tangled in her hair. "Would you *please* come home with me tonight? And then spend the day with me tomorrow? I promise to feed you and water you and tend to your every whim and desire." I press a kiss to her forehead this time and her cheeks flush as I pull away.

"Every whim and desire, huh?" She wiggles her eyebrows at me dramatically and giggles. Oh, she thinks I'm kidding. Now that I've had a taste of her, this polite public flirting and texting could never be enough. I lean forward, eyes darkening, and slip my hand back around to the front of her throat.

"Every. Single. One." I punctuate each word with a tap of my thumb right over her pulse. I smirk as I feel her thighs clench around mine, but she's interrupted by another yawn, followed shortly by my own. "Alright, let's get going before we both pass out on this couch."

We gather the rest of our clothes and toss the trash from our snack binge before I head to the back and shut everything off. I drive us back to my apartment and find her the smallest t-shirt I own to sleep in. Seeing her standing in my bedroom doorway, hair mussed and legs bare, is poetically surreal. It's like she was plucked from a renaissance painting and dropped right into my apartment.

I pull back my blanket and hold out a hand to her. The second she takes it, I yank her into the bed next to me, my body curling around hers. I bury my face in her hair and pull the blanket over us, and she snuggles closer into my grip. Barely a breath later, we're both passed out.

When I dream, I'm back in the village. We've defeated the bandits who took over the town, and the party is celebrating with the townsfolk at what's left of the inn before the long work of repairing the damage begins tomorrow morning. Everyone heads out to find a safe place to sleep for the night, and the blonde warrior woman takes my hand. She leads me to the kitchen and lifts a trapdoor, grabbing a candle and descending into the darkness.

I follow her down and take in the musty wine cellar. There are boxes of food supplies in one corner, racks of wine bottles and large unmarked barrels along the back wall. In the middle of the floor is a nest of grain sacks covered in blankets. Some are singed on the edges, and I remember that she had disappeared earlier in the night. She must have been salvaging things from the upper rooms that had been damaged in the fires.

I watch her from the ladder as she sets the candle on a crate and curls up on the makeshift bed. "Come, warrior," she whispers in her thick accent, patting the empty space next to her. "You did good today. Rest. There is more to do tomorrow." I nod and kick off my boots before settling in. She turns to me and lays a hand on my chest. Just as she opens her mouth to speak, I wake up.

Callie breathes softly, my arm still wrapped around her and her legs still twisted in mine. We barely moved all night. I gently pull my hand out from under her head and untangle myself. She stirs but doesn't wake, so I tuck the blanket back around her and go make coffee.

I drop into my chair at the desk in the corner of the bedroom and pull out my notebook, but I can't seem to drag my eyes away from her. She's facing me, her hair poking out at odd angles from under the blanket that she's got tucked up to her chin. Her mouth hangs open, and I can hear her soft little snores from here. I take a sip of my coffee and almost choke on it when she speaks.

'Quit staring at me, creep," she mutters, her lips curling up as she cracks one eye open. I roll my eyes at her.

"Yeah, yeah. Good morning to you too. Coffee?" She responds with an unintelligible grunt that sounds vaguely affirmative, so I head to the kitchen and return with a second cup. We stop at a drive-thru for more coffee and some breakfast before heading to Strikers to clean up from last night. After a quick stop at her apartment for a change of clothes, we end up back at my apartment just in time for lunch.

I stick a frozen pizza in the oven for us and offer the shower to Callie while it cooks. She grabs my hand and drags me in with her. The pizza is burnt to a crisp when we're done, so we toss it and have cereal.

The rest of the afternoon is spent in companionable silence, me writing at my desk and her curled up on my bed reading a book she claimed from my shelf. I periodically bounce ideas off of her, and we talk through some decisions I'm struggling to make in my story. I'm writing the scene that I dreamt about last night, and I want to ask her if I should add some spice to this story or just fade to black. I'm going over the wording in my head so I don't sound like a fucking loser when it comes out of my mouth when Callie speaks up.

"Might as well add it," she mumbles, not looking up from her book.

"Uh... huh?" My eyes narrow in her direction, eyebrows bunching in confusion. Did I ask that out loud? No, I don't think I did.

The bookmark she's twirling in her fingers stops abruptly and her panicked gaze shoots to mine. "Um, I... Well, I'm not sure... " She stumbles over her words, like she's trying to figure out which ones will make me stop asking questions. She sticks the bookmark back in her book and sets it on the bed with a heavy sigh, but still says nothing.

"Callie," I say, my voice deceptively calm. "What just happened?"

She tips her head back and closes her eyes, another heavy sigh leaving her before she speaks again, just one word.

"Fuck."

Chapter Eleven

"Callie, what the fuck?" She flinches when I stand up from my chair and I immediately regret my harsh tone. "Please," I ask, softer this time. "Please explain how the fuck you answered a question I asked you in my head." I take a few slow steps toward the bed and sit down on the opposite end from her.

"I..." she starts, closing her eyes again. "I can't explain, because you're not going to believe me anyway." Her words are rushed, like she had to force them out.

"Callie, are you kidding me? Look around you." I gesture around us, from the bookshelf full of fantasy books to the vintage Hobbit and Star Wars posters framed on my wall. "What exactly do you think you're going to tell me that I won't at least entertain the validity of?"

She considers for a moment before her shoulders droop in concession. "I'm not supposed to interfere," she whispers, her voice cracking.

"Hey, come here," I mutter, pulling her into my lap. I tuck the stray hairs behind her ear and trail my fingers along her jaw, tipping her chin up gently until her eyes pierce into mine. "You can tell me anything."

With one more deep exhale, she finally caves. "I'm going to tell you some things, and I need you to know before I do that..." She pauses, swallowing. "You're talented on your own. What I'm going to tell you doesn't change that." I'm so confused, but I nod anyway. That seems to satisfy her, so she continues.

"Callie is short for Calliope. As in Ancient Greek muse Calliope. I mean, I'm not *her*, but I'm named after her," she rushes out. I squint at her, not sure what being named after a muse has to do with anything. "She's a great great something aunt. But I'm a muse. It's all a bit bureaucratic these days, but it's still very much an indentured servitude and we're all just born into it without any real say. Anyway, I was assigned to you. That's why I'm here. I'm supposed to inspire you to write your book."

She finally stops to breathe, and I stare at her for a beat before I blurt out the stupidest shit I could think of apparently.

"By what, fucking me?"

"What? No!" She jumps back like I slapped her, and I wish I could shove my words back in my mouth and choke on them. "I... That is *not* part of the job. This is... different. *We're* different."

I groan and drop my forehead into my hand. "I'm so sorry," I tell her. "That was shitty and uncalled for. I don't know why I said it." She stares at me, mouth open, like no one's ever apologized to her before. "I'm sorry," I say again, barely audible. She says nothing but she nods lightly.

I'm not sure what to say to any of this. If I open my mouth again, I'm sure I'll just put my foot in it. I don't see a reason for her to lie to me about what she is, but it's all a little hard to believe. I decide to see it scientifically. I'll need more evidence before drawing a conclusion.

"Okay, tell me more," I urge. "What does that all mean?" She releases a relieved breath before continuing.

"Well, we get assigned randomly to anyone the Fates see a thread for. People with talents they haven't discovered, people who struggle to find success..." Her eyes drift up to meet mine. "People with lots of talent but not enough motivation."

Ouch. "I'm guessing I fall under that last category?" Her gaze drifts to the floor as she nods. "No, it's okay. It's not an incorrect assessment, I guess." She gives me an apologetic smile.

"So, when we get assigned, we just follow whatever the Fates tell us to do to get into your path. There's a whole dossier and everything."

"Oh, I have *got* to see that." The world's most boring case file, I'm sure. "So, what about you hearing me? How does that play in?"

"I wasn't lying to you. I *am* actually mostly deaf. Not a muse thing, just a me thing. But, while you're my charge, I can kind of hear your thoughts." My eyes widen in horror. *Oh fuck, all those times I thought about...*

"Not every thought, I swear!" She interrupts my impending panic attack, but I'm still mortified. "I can only hear things related to your inspiration. Like if you have writer's block, or if you're struggling to connect with a character or make a plot decision or something. I can hear it like an echo in my head, and I can step in to adjust or provide more inspiration as needed. Like I said, we're not supposed to interfere directly, so being able to hear your thoughts about your work makes it easier to inspire you."

I nod my head slowly while I try to process everything she just dumped on me while she eyes me warily. "Are you trying to figure out how to get the crazy lady out of your apartment?" she asks with a nervous laugh.

Am I? It's hard to believe that she's not making this up - or maybe that she's just batshit crazy - but it all kind of lines up. Ever since she showed up in town, I've had the motivation and the inspiration to plot out and start writing an entire novel. The dreams, the annotations... Wait a minute.

"I knew it was you," I blurt out. Her eyebrows scrunch together. "The annotated books. The purple pen in those used books you were giving me. I thought it was just a coincidence at first, but then I opened one in the store, and it had nothing in it. The writing appeared as soon as I got to work. That was you, right?"

"Yeah," she nods, her expression almost bashful. "Those are all books from my personal collection actually. The annotations aren't just magic; they're my own notes."

Of course they are. Of fucking course it was her own words and ideas that inspired me to come up with a whole world of my own. It dawns on me that I never actually told her about the annotations magically appearing in the book, just that they were there. I was going to tell her after last night, but I hadn't gotten around to it yet. She wouldn't have even known about them unless she had something to do with them one way or another.

"Okay," I say with a sigh. "Let's say this is all true and I believe you. Why is this," I point a finger back and forth between us. "Different?"

"We're not supposed to interfere," she says again. "That means we just show up in your life close enough to provide the inspiration. New barista at your local coffee shop, new coworker in your office... New bookseller at your favorite bookstore. Once you've written your first book, recorded your first album, painted your first masterpiece, whatever the assignment is, we disappear." My stomach twists at that last word. I'm sure my face does too, because she rushes to elaborate. "You're not even supposed to remember me. I was supposed to just move out of town after the job was done. We're not supposed to get... attached."

I can't help myself. I pull her closer and shoot her a grin. "You're attached to me, huh," I chide, wiggling my eyebrows. She laughs, and warmth spreads through me. I hate to drag the moment down, but I have to know. "So why did you? Get attached?"

She looks away again, pink flushing her cheeks. "I'm not sure, honestly. When you first talked to me at the bookstore, I tried to be polite and distant, but I couldn't help myself. I haven't been on many assignments, and they're usually all too oblivious to notice me. But you saw me immediately, and you were obviously so nervous to talk to me. It was cute."

I sigh. Cute is the last thing I was going for, but if it works, it works. I guess.

"Well, I'm not saying I don't believe you. Honestly, it makes a lot of sense, despite being absolutely off the fucking wall. Not to mention the implications that, if you're a real muse, then the whole Greek pantheon is...?" She nods slowly in confirmation, and I can feel the slow transformation from brain matter into soup as I try to process that information. "Yeah, we'll get to that shit later when my brain is solid matter again."

"I'm sorry. I know it's a lot," she mutters, eyes on the floor again. Wetness pools in the corners of them. "I'm a lot." Those three words shatter any hope I had of holding on to my anger about this secret.

"Hey," I say, pulling her chin gently to face me. "You're not a lot. You are who you are, and *what* you are, and that's the perfect amount. This situation might be a lot, but you're perfect. Anyone who thinks you're 'a lot' can go find less and fucking choke on it."

When she looks up at me, her eyes are spilling over but her mouth is curling into a smile, so hopefully that was the right thing to say. I swipe my thumb at the tear falling down her cheek and lean in to capture her lips with mine. Her arms slide around the back of my neck, and she nestles her face into my chest, tears soaking my shirt.

She stays there for a few minutes before pulling back, mumbling something I can't understand. Despite everything, I let out a low chuckle. "Baby, I can't understand a single fucking thing you're saying right now," I tell her, brushing hair out of her face. She sniffs and tries again.

"They're going to reassign me if they find out," she says, and all of a sudden, I can't fucking breathe. "It's not like anyone monitors us when we're on assignments, but if I don't come back, they'll notice.

"What does that mean? They take you from me and send you to someone else?" She nods, her bottom lip quivering. My grip around her waist tightens like that's going to stop a fucking deity from yanking her out of my life. I feel myself going into manic mode. "So, what do we do? Can we stop it? Hide from them? What if we run?"

"There's no hiding or running. They'll find us. Well, they'll find *me*. I'm tied to my contract, and it's basically like a magical GPS." One hand drops to her lap in defeat, the other clinging to the back of my neck. "The only way out is if someone buys my contract, which has never happened before." Now I'm seeing red.

"What do you mean, 'buys your contract'? For what? How much value do they place on your fucking life?" I can feel my voice getting louder and rein it in with a deep breath. "What's the cost?" I'm mentally tallying what I have in my account as if it's going to be enough because all I can do is grasp at straws at this point. How am I supposed to stop the fucking Greek pantheon from taking my girlfriend?

Huh. Girlfriend? *Probably ought to discuss that at some point.*

"No," she mutters softly, laying a hand on my cheek. "I... It's not a monetary price, Devon. And it's never the same thing, but the price is *always* too high. He'll demand whatever is most important to you, and if you try to back out, he'll just kill you instead." I'm silent for a moment, wading through my immediate thoughts and the repercussions of voicing them before I finally answer.

Fuck it.

"And what if the most important thing to me is you?" Her mouth falls open in stunned silence, but I continue. "I know we haven't known each other for that long, and this whole thing is one big extenuating circumstance, but I didn't exactly have much going on before you got here. In case you can't tell," I say, gesturing around the room. "I don't get out much. I don't have many friends, and they're all just a step above an acquaintance. I don't have any immediate family left, and literally all of my hobbies share a main goal of escaping reality. I've really just been floating through life like a ghost until you showed up."

She squeezes her eyes shut and more waiting tears fall from the corners. She sniffs, wiping them away and meeting my gaze again before I continue.

"It doesn't really matter to me if you were sent here to be my muse. Even if it wasn't your job, you'd be my muse. You were dealt a shitty hand, and you still play it with a smile. Watching your face light up is like switching from an old black and white TV to 4K. I don't need whatever power you have to inspire me to write. All I need is you, laying in my bed while I bounce ideas off of you. A few weeks ago, I was just... existing. Haunting an empty apartment with all the lights off." I cradle her face in my hands. "Since you got here, it's like someone turned all the lights on and threw a party.

All I need is you and the way you're looking at me right now."

She stares at me with gleaming eyes for the longest minute of my life before tugging on the back of my neck, dragging my face to hers as our lips crash together. When she pulls back, her eyes meet mine with a new resolve.

"I won't let you suffer to free me," she says firmly. "The cost will be too high and I'm... I'm not worth it."

My gaze hardens at her bullshit words. "Who told you that you're not worth it?"

"I... well...," she stammers, tripping over filler words to avoid the real answer.

"Look, I don't know how this works, and I don't really care, but there's nothing I have now that I wouldn't give up in a heartbeat to keep you to myself. So, make a call or a summoning circle or whatever you need to do, and let me talk to the fucker who thinks he can place a value on you."

It occurs to me that maybe she doesn't *want* me to buy out her contract, so I add, "If that's what you want, anyway. I just assumed..."

"Yes!" She nods emphatically. "I just... I don't want anything bad to happen to you because of me." Her eyebrows knit together, and I can tell this is making her uneasy. It's obvious that no one has ever really given a shit about her. Not like she deserves, anyway.

"Look, nothing is going to happen to me," I assure her. "And if it does, good or bad, it'll be the first thing to happen to me in a long time either way. I'm done just existing, and I don't think I can really *live* without you around. Make the call." I press a kiss to her forehead.

"Okay," she says finally, placing a hand on my chest. "But not yet. I want you to be able to finish your book first. At least the first draft."

My eyes narrow on her. She's putting way too much faith

in my abilities here. "How fast do you think I write, Callie? I also have a job to go to, and so do you."

She barks out a laugh, and I realize how dumb the last part was. "Part of the job is having the ability to show up - *and disappear* - without anyone remembering I was ever there in the first place. As for your job, you've got like a billion hours of PTO saved up, right?" Before I can open my mouth to protest, she lays a finger over my lips. "That's not a muse thing; I'm just inferring from context clues. Take your vacation. If they give you a hard time, I'll work some magic and make it happen. Then I'll disappear and hole up with you here until it's done."

I consider her offer. It sounds like a good plan, honestly. And I do have at least a month of PTO saved up. They won't be happy about it, but whatever. If I lose my momentum without her muse gifts, at least I'll have one good book under my belt. If that's the only thing I ever get published, then we'll figure something else out.

I can be a one hit wonder with a day job. We can travel, and she can show me all the places she's lived. *Been assigned*, I remind myself, and now I'm pissed off all over again. Who the fuck came up with this vile system where she's born into servitude? How is that right?

She pulls me out of my head, one hand sliding up the back of my neck to tangle in my hair.

"What do you say? I'm nothing if not a takeout-powered idea machine," she chides with an impish smile.

"Yeah, okay," I concede. "First draft first." She graces me with a radiant smile before throwing her arms around me and we both fall back into the bed.

Chapter Twelve

We spend the rest of the day curled up in a nest of blankets. We read in silence for a while, and then Callie regales me with tales of her previous charges. Apparently, muses have specialties, and hers is the written word. Her last assignment was a fiction writer who was working on a post-apocalyptic piece that was meant to be a warning statement about the current administration, and he was having trouble finding someone willing to publish it. Callie's job was to inspire him to change up the writing enough that it wasn't glaringly obvious.

We're still nested in the blankets when it starts to get dark outside, so I order us some dinner.

Callie jumps when my doorbell rings. My phone goes off at the same time, letting me know that our food is here. I bring everything into the bedroom and step back out to the kitchen to grab drinks and paper towels. When I come back, she's got little white takeout containers lined up on my desk. She opens one with what I'm guessing is wontons based on the little happy dance she does in the beanbag chair I dragged in from the living room for her. She glances up at me in the doorway, and waves me over to eat.

"If you don't take some of these now, I'm going to inhale them before you even get a whiff," she warns, plucking a crispy wonton out of the container.

"You sure about that?" I ask, snatching it out of her fingers just before she takes a bite and leaning in to steal a kiss. She slaps my chest and steals the wonton back before I can shove it in my mouth. I come around the desk and sink into my chair, starting in on a container of sesame chicken. Once she's got enough food in her for her stomach to stop rumbling, we pick up where we left off.

"So, how many assignments have you been on?" It feels like asking someone for their body count, but I have to know.

"Maybe a hundred or so," she says. "I lost count. Not nearly as many as some of the others. I think my favorite assignment was Mr. Alighieri," she says, absentmindedly poking at her rice. My brows knit together as I try to remember why that name sounds familiar. "He was kind of boring, but Florence was *beautiful* in the 1200s." The chicken falls from my chopsticks halfway to my mouth as I gape at her.

"I'm sorry, 1200s," I choke out. "As in, the century?" She freezes, giving me a sheepish smile like she didn't just drop a bomb on me. I blink at her a few times, mouth still hanging open like an idiot, and then I open my mouth to let yet another stupid fucking question roll out of it. "Exactly how old *are* you?" I cringe as soon as I say it. I need a fucking muzzle.

Her lips roll into a thin line, and she puffs her cheeks out for a second with a deep breath before letting it out in a slow stream. "Well," she starts, fidgeting with the hem of the hoodie she's claimed as her own instead of answering. I raise an expectant eyebrow at her, and she lets out a heavy sigh. "I don't know *exactly* how old I am, honestly. I remember my first assignment was a woman named Rabia from Persia."

I pull out my phone and search for "Rabia Persia writer", not expecting much, but a Wiki article pops up. "Rabia Balkhi," I read aloud, and Callie jumps forward. "That's her!" she shouts, so I continue. "...Also known as Rabia al-Quzdari, was a... tenth... century..." My words slow to a halt as my eyes drift up to her. "Tenth century," I repeat. "As in 900 AD." It's not a question, but I wait for her to confirm it anyway.

"Yeah, that sounds about right," she says, pushing a grain of rice around the bottom of the container. "It was later in the tenth, though, so I'm like... just over a thousand I guess?"

Cool, cool. Yeah, nothing fucking bonkers about that. It's fine. I take a second to compose myself before I say something that actually offends her.

"Okay, that leads me to my next question. What's the uh... the lifespan of a muse? Like where are you at on the age scale? Toddler, teenager, adult...?"

She hums, scrunching up her eyebrows as she does immortality math. Fucking hell.

"Well, I don't think there's really a solid number? I think the oldest muse I know is the first Calliope, and I remember her saying she was about 900 when Mount Vesuvius erupted, so she's got to be like 3,000 at least." I let out a low whistle. "So, I guess, in comparison, I'm like 25 in human years." I purse my lips and nod slowly. I can work with that. That's something I can wrap my head around, like dog years.

"I don't know of any muses who have ever actually died, now that I think about it. There have been a few who were killed, but we don't really age much, and we don't get sick." Her lips tilt up. "Guess you're stuck with me for a while, huh?"

"Well," I say quietly. "I'm stuck with you for as long as you're stuck with me." It takes a second for my words to sink in, but I know it clicks when her gaze whips to me. Her lips part, but she says nothing, just looks down at her lap. "Sorry," I mumble, reaching across the desk to take her hand in mine. I pull it up to my face, pressing a kiss to each knuckle. "Didn't mean to pop your bubble."

"No, you're right. A problem for another day?" She gives me a questioning look that turns into a small smile when I nod.

"Yeah, another day," I agree, and mentally file that thought away under 'future shitstorms'. "Okay, I don't want you to take this the wrong way, but I have a question." She narrows her eyes on me, and I hope like hell that this comes out as curiosity and not offense. "If you're a thousand years old, how is there literally anything you haven't experienced? You said you'd never been bowling before, and you were so excited to meet the cows... I just... How is anything a new thing for you?"

"Well, like I said, I haven't been on a ton of assignments. I've been told I'm not a very good muse," she mumbles the last bit, cringing. I take her hand and squeeze silently, giving her the space to process what she wants to say. "Anyway, I only get to experience a tiny bit of the lives I get assigned to. I was assigned to a farmer's son once, and I basically just had to hide out in his barn because he never left the property. Most of my assignments in recent decades were spent making coffee, honestly."

My blood boils for her again, but I tamper down the rage. This isn't about me right now. "What about when you're not on an assignment?"

"The best of the muses live on Mount Helicon. It's like the hub for muse society. They have apartments and technology and lives, but they spend most of their time on assignments and don't actually get to enjoy any of it. The rest of us are housed on Mount Parnassus, which is basically just empty farmland and dormitories. We train our powers and do chores and that's about it. Some of them form little cliques and spend their downtime together, but I've never been into all of that. We have a library, so I mostly just read."

Ah, that explains a lot. I want to ask about a million more questions, but I don't think I can bear her looking this sad anymore.

"So, about these powers," I start, hoping for a subject change. "Do you control them directly, or do you just think of what you want, and they make it happen?"

"Well, I mostly have control of them. If I want something to happen, it does. Sometimes, our magic just makes things happen, though. Like I choose my clothes in my head, and they change. But if I were to want to change but not make a conscious choice about my outfit, it just defaults to something I've worn previously."

"So, wait, your clothes aren't real?" I'm struggling to wrap my head around this much fuckery in one sitting, which is insane considering how much magic-based media I've consumed in my life.

"No, they're real," she says with a giggle. "They're just not always the same clothes, or even clothes at all, if that makes sense? Alchemical magic is matter-based, so what I'm currently wearing turns into what I want to wear. Say we went to Strikers and there were no bowling balls left at all. I could take off my jacket and make it a bowling ball and then turn it back into a jacket when we left."

"No fucking way," I blurt out. Call me Eddie, because that was fucking *eloquent*. She raises an eyebrow at the challenge before slipping my hoodie over her head. When she pops her head out from under the hem, bright purple hair sticks out in all directions. I bark out a laugh because what the fuck else am I supposed to say to that? As she pulls her arms out, I see that her t-shirt and sleep shorts are now a light purple dress. The one she was wearing the first time I walked into the store, actually.

"Holy shit," I whisper, and she lets out a cackle. She pulls the hoodie back on and I shoot out of my seat so I can watch the change. The bottom of her dress morphs back into her shorts like, well... like *magic*. I rub my eyes hard like a fucking cartoon character, half expecting her to disappear like a transient hallucination, but she's still sitting there, hair pale blonde again, face split into a wide grin.

"Okay, wait. That's not even the best part." She holds up a fortune cookie from the desk in front of my face. "What is your absolute favorite kind of cookie?"

"Um..." I think I know where this is going, and I'm debating between letting her show off and trying to trip her up. I decide to land somewhere in the middle. "Salted caramel macaron," I say with a smirk. She opens the cellophane around the cookie in midair and, when it plops out onto the desk, it's the most perfectly shaped caramel-colored macaron I've ever seen in my life. She picks it up and cracks it in half, handing me a piece and scarfing the other down herself.

I'm still staring at my piece when she huffs out a laugh. "You can eat it. It won't bite," she tells me. I shake my head a bit and focus my gaze on her before popping it in my mouth.

"This is the best fucking macaron I've ever had," I mumble around the bite, and she beams at me. "Can you make anything you want?"

"Well, there are definitely limits. Like I could probably change that into any kind of cookie you asked for as long as I knew what it was. I couldn't turn it into a full five course dinner, though. It has to be..."

"An equivalent exchange?" I interrupt her, wiggling my eyebrows at the reference. I realize too late that an immortal being who lives on a mountain probably hasn't seen *Fullmetal*

Alchemist, but at least I can appreciate my own joke. Then she shocks the absolute shit out of me.

"Well, to obtain, something of equal value must be lost. Obviously," she says with a smirk. *Well, fuck.* "The library is a full collection of past and present written works. That includes manga," she explains.

"Aren't you just full of surprises," I say, tossing the trash in the takeout bag and clearing some space for my notebook. "So... about this first draft."

We spend the next few days brainstorming, writing, and nesting. I've written another twenty chapters or so, and I've got six more planned to wrap everything up. I'm so close I can taste it, and now I'm terrified to finish it. What if they take her from me anyway? What if, no matter what we do, I lose her? What the fuck am I supposed to do against literal gods?

The next morning, I insist on taking a break and typing up what I have written so far instead of writing more. I tell her it's because my hand is cramping from all the writing, which isn't a lie. I probably should have been typing this all to begin with. Callie eyes me suspiciously at the suggestion, but her qualms are quickly forgotten when I set a full home cooked breakfast spread and coffee in front of her. I bring my laptop in from the living room and spend all afternoon typing, occasionally tossing lines out at her for critique.

She spends the day curled up in my bed reading again, surrounded by a nest of blankets and snacks. I go back and forth between my desk and the bed, trying to be productive enough that she doesn't notice I'm dragging my feet. I'm not sure if it's just her presence or if she's actively using her powers on me, but I'm continuously getting new ideas as I type up my own words. Different ways to word things, minor details to expound on... This story seems to get better with every addition and change.

By the time we reconvene at my desk to scarf down some

dinner, I'm a little over halfway done typing everything up. It was something I'd have to do eventually, but it was doubling as a procrastination effort and it's quickly outliving its plausibility.

"It's not as good as real Italian food," she says, pushing the remnants of a meatball around her nearly empty plate. "But it was pretty damn good." She leans back in her chair and pats a hand on her stomach with a groan that I've learned indicates an incoming food coma. Sure enough, she crawls back into bed and dozes off while I take a break from typing to play some video games.

I choose a simple 16-bit farming sim to give my brain a break, but it just keeps spinning in circles around all the insane information I've crammed into it over the last week. Gods are real. Greek mythology is real. Muses are real. Magic is real. *Callie* is real, and mine, and laying in my bed, and I'm... not in it with her? *Because I'm a fucking idiot, right.*

I abandon my game, sliding out of my sweats and slipping under the blanket behind her. I press a kiss to the side of her neck, and she hums. I can see the corner of her mouth tip up in her sleep, so I plant another one there before burying my face in her hair and pulling her tight to me. There's no way in hell I'll be able to sleep, but being wrapped around her like this calms my nerves enough to stop the tailspin I was putting myself into.

I need a plan.

We've been so wrapped up in my book that we haven't left the apartment in days. The weather is supposed to be tolerable tomorrow, and the farm is open all day for the general public. I'll take her to go see the cows, and then we can get Mexican for dinner. That should eat up most of the day. I'm sure I can think of some other *extracurricular activities* to take up the evening. We can fill up on dinner, but I'm sure I'll still be starving for her.

Chapter Thirteen

As soon as we pull into the parking lot, we're stopped by a teenager in a reflective vest. He holds a little orange cone in his hand, halting incoming traffic to let an employee walk one of the cows from the barns to the petting area. She's got a little fleece coat laid over her back with her name embroidered on it. Callie is literally vibrating with excitement in the passenger seat, and I can't help the grin that spreads across my face when I glance over at her.

"Her name is Daisy," she whispers, her hands balled in little fists in her lap. I suspect it's to keep her from jumping out of the car and running for Daisy.

Once Daisy has been safely escorted to the petting area, we park and head in. There's a hot cocoa table set up outside of the barn, so I grab a cup for each of us while Callie waits in line by the outdoor heaters. Despite being perfectly capable of morphing her clothes into something warmer, she insisted on stealing one of my old high school hoodies. Something about seeing her wearing my clothes makes me a little bit feral, so I'm not complaining.

When I join her in line, we're next to go in. She inhales her first gulp of hot chocolate and immediately sucks cold air in to soothe her burnt mouth.

"It's literally in the name," I laugh. "*Hot* cocoa." She sticks her bright red tongue out at me, and I pull her head towards me, pressing a kiss to her temple. She takes another sip, smaller this time, and her grimace turns to a grin. The elderly woman at the door waves us forward and Callie beams at me.

There are cows lined up at the inner fence, ready for their scritches and treats. A young girl with 4H patches on her jacket walks around with a calf on a harness, supervising her while she butts her head into any available hand. Callie pounces on the opportunity, crouching down to run her hands over the calf's fuzzy snout and scratching behind her ears.

We spend a little under an hour in the barn before Callie's nose starts to turn red. I'm having fun just watching her enjoy herself, but she's got to be freezing by now. She's deep in conversation with one of the cows behind the fence, so I slip my hand into the one hanging at her side and tug lightly until she's facing me.

"I think you've successfully made friends with every cow in the barn," I tell her. "You ready to get some food? Next stop on the Seven Wonders tour is full of tacos." She glances over her shoulder at the cow for a moment before turning back to me.

"I suppose," she says slowly, pointing a finger at me with a stern glare. "But we *will* be coming back to see all my new friends." She squints at me until I nod in agreement. As if I could deny her anything. A smile breaks out across her face, and she surges up on her tiptoes to plant a kiss on my cheek.

We head back to town and grab some lunch at the Mexican restaurant. We get a whole sampler feast, from chips and queso all the way to deep fried ice cream and a bunch of things in between that I can't hope to pronounce properly. She orders it all for us, expertly and in Spanish, because of fucking course she can speak Spanish. I can tell when she really likes whatever she's eating because she does her little happy dance in her seat, and I want to make her feel like that all the time.

When we're so full I think they're going to have to roll us out the door, we pack up the leftovers in boxes and go home.

Home. My apartment has always been more than just a place to live. Somewhere I was comfortable, where I could take the mask off and just exist in peace. It's spacious enough for me and all my stuff. Even with all the things I like to collect, I haven't run out of room. Everything in it is conveniently placed, and the kitchen is big enough for me to comfortably cook in.

The living room has enough room for my bookshelves and display cases. My furniture is comfortable, and I think I did a pretty good job decorating the walls and end tables. I've lived there since about a week after my mom died, when I got evicted from the house because our landlord said the lease was "with her and not me". Fucking scumbag.

Growing up, Mom made sure that I always had the freedom to do whatever weird shit my little heart desired. We didn't have much after my dad left, aside from the months he actually remembered to send child support, but she made the best out of it. It never even dawned on me that we had less than anyone else until I was old enough to go to other people's houses. I never really cared about what we had or the box it was in. Home was my mom, and then she died, so I had to create a new home.

Now, though? If my apartment burnt down tonight, I'd still have a home. It's sitting in my passenger seat, bouncing around to the music streaming out of the car speakers loud enough that she can hear it and swooning at me like I hung the fucking moon for her. It's following me through the door, fingers entwined with mine, barely making it to the counter to drop the leftovers before she's wrapping her arms around me from behind and squeezing. It's staring up at me with big blue eyes as I turn in her grip and leaning down to kiss her for the millionth time today.

Callie is my home now, and I'm not letting anyone, anything, or any *stupid fucking god* take her from me. I'm done trying to buy time. It's time to make a plan.

We spend the rest of the night bouncing ideas around for the ending of my book. I can feel her influence on me like a warm trickle down the back of my neck, words flowing freely from my brain to the page. My writing isn't the only thing she's inspiring, though. We work until well past midnight, and I wait until we're curled up in bed to say anything about the plan I've been formulating all evening.

"So," I start, tapping my fingers nervously where they lay on my stomach. Her head is nestled into my shoulder, one arm laid across my chest. "We're just about done with the first draft. I think we should talk about the plan." She hums noncommittally, snuggling closer into me with no response. Shit, I should have waited until morning. I should have-

"There's no planning when it comes to them," she interrupts my spiraling, her voice quiet and steady. "They do what they want, and they make decisions on whims. Once you're done with your draft, I'll send a message to Apollo."

I'm sorry, who? Yeah, we're going to be circling back to that later.

"He'll set a time to meet up with us and we'll petition him for my contract. He'll name some outrageous price and expect us to either give in or haggle with him. If you try to haggle, he might let you. Or he might kill you for defying him. Depends on how he's feeling that day. If you decide you're willing to pay the final price, then he'll take payment, and I'll belong to you. If the price is too high..."

She sniffs quietly, her fingers tracing the tattoo on my

shoulder lightly. When she doesn't continue, I take her fingers with my free hand and bring it to my mouth, pressing a kiss to each knuckle. She lets out a heavy sigh before starting again.

"If you decide I'm not worth the price, they'll reassign-" My gaze whips to her.

"Woah," I stop her, sitting up as much as I can without tossing her. Now that I can see her face, I can see the tears forming in her eyes and the sad smile. I swipe my thumb across her cheek, catching the first tear as it falls. "I need you to listen to me, and I need you to absorb what I'm saying. There's no price I wouldn't pay for you to be mine. There's not a single thing I have that I wouldn't be willing to give up for you to be free."

Her eyes meet mine, and I can feel the pain behind them like it's my own. "I won't let you suffer to save me," she whispers.

"I won't let you suffer to save myself," I retort. "Let me decide what I can and can't handle, because you're worth it to me. You're worth more than anything I have. I don't care if he wants every penny I have or everything I own. Take my sight, or my voice, or years off of my life. Callie, I don't give a single fuck what he wants, as long as it ends with you in my arms every night for the rest of our lives."

"For the rest of *your* life." I tense at her words. They're so quiet I almost don't hear them. "I don't age, Devon. You'll grow old and you'll die, and I'll still be *this*." She gestures down at herself. *This* meaning a thousand-year-old muse in the body of a 25-year-old woman. "You'll get older, and people will see us and think I'm your daughter, and then your granddaughter. And then one day, when you die, I'll be all alone again." Her breathing is fast and shallow, like she's working herself into a panic attack.

"Hey, relax" I murmur, brushing her hair down and pressing a kiss to her temple. After a few deep breaths, I can feel her settle back into my side as her breathing returns to normal. "Once we get through the first step, we'll worry about the next one. For now, let's just worry about the deal. Tell me what to expect. Are we talking *Apollo* Apollo? Like, God of the Sun Apollo?"

"Yeah, and he's a fucking dick." Her face is so serious, but I can't help the laugh that escapes me. She pins me with a glare for a second before it softens and she giggles along with me.

"I'm sorry, did you just call a god a fucking dick? Isn't that smite-worthy or something?"

"Only if I say it to his face," she says with a smirk. "And he knows he is, anyway. He's just the *worst*. He's impulsive and rude and, honestly, he's kind of a creep. He likes to think he's in charge of the muses because he's a god and he had a kid with Calliope a million years ago. As if you can walk anywhere in Olympus without tripping over a demigod. It doesn't help that some Russian composer in the twenties wrote a whole ballet calling him 'Leader of the Muses'. But, because he's a nepo baby who gets whatever he wants, Zeus made him the mediator for all of our petitions, and he gets the final say on anything we do."

I nod slowly in lieu of a response. She just referred to the god who drags the sun across the sky as a creep *and* a nepo baby. Although, based on what I know about Greek mythology, she's probably not wrong. I take a deep breath. I have a feeling this isn't going to go as smoothly as I'd hoped.

"Great," I mumble on an exhale. "Piece of cake."

Chapter Fourteen

We spend the next two days finishing the first draft. Most of them, anyway. It takes every ounce of self-control I have not to drag her into my bed with me and never leave. We can just hide there forever, right?

Unfortunately, I begrudgingly remind myself that, as much as I'd love to disappear with her, she'd still be tied to them. As soon as they realize she's no longer "on the clock", they'll be here in a heartbeat to drag her away. No, she needs to be free. She *deserves* to be free.

So, we finish the book.

I have two completely different ideas for the path to take, and she has me write them both out and read them to her. We decide on the climax that was hopefully unexpected, sad but not too painful, and a relatively happy ending. The rest of the story was a little darker, so I wanted to end on a lighter note. Especially since this could be my only book.

Surprisingly, that thought hasn't bothered me as much as I thought it would. We've been operating under the assumption that my ability to write is what Apollo will demand as payment, so I've decided to start coming to terms with that in advance.

Now, sitting at my desk, typing up the last paragraph, it's starting to sink in. There's a weight in my chest that gets heavier the closer I get to the end. I've loved writing my whole life. I've always been able to escape into my own worlds, but I could never get something like this down on paper. There was always something missing, some integral ingredient to the mix that turned all the pieces into one cohesive unit.

I think Callie was that missing link.

I know she was sent here to be that link. Logically, that makes sense. She was sent here to be the motivation that helped me put pen to paper, to string my words together and weave them into a world that I can share with others. That's her *job*, and it's not like she had a choice in the matter anyway.

I thought I'd be more broken up about it, but I'm finding that I really don't give a fuck. I wouldn't have been able to finish this story without her to begin with. If buying her freedom means that I don't ever get to experience this again, then so be it. She's worth the cost and then some. We'll figure the rest out later.

Callie is passed out, buried under a pile of blankets on the bed. I type everything but the last word before I slip under the blanket, molding my front to her back and sliding my hands around her waist. She stirs, a tiny moan escaping as she stretches out like a cat.

"Hey," she whispers, turning around in my arms.

"Hey." I press a kiss to the tip of her nose, trailing them down the side of her face. "I thought you might want to be awake for the last word."

Her eyes widen. "All done?" The excitement in her voice is tinged with something bitter, and I know she's worried about what comes next.

"Mhm," I confirm, burying my face in the crook of her

neck and giving her one more good squeeze before rolling off the bed and plopping back down at my desk. She hops up and follows me, crowding close behind me to watch the last word.

"H... O..." I read the letters out loud, as dramatically as possible, as she giggles nervously behind me. "M... E... Period." As soon as I type the period, I spin my chair to face her, and she steps between my knees. Three months to finish what I spent my whole life trying to do, all thanks to her.

"You did it!" She glides her hands along my shoulders, clasping them behind my neck.

"*We* did it," I correct her, skating my hands up the backs of her thighs. She beams down at me, and I tuck my head against her side. *Now what?* The words hang in the air, but I don't dare say them. I won't fool myself into thinking she's changed her mind about doing this. I haven't either, but maybe we can get one more day before we have to face reality.

I press a kiss to her ribcage, and she inhales softly, running her fingers through the hair at my nape. Another kiss, lower this time. Another at her hip. Each elicits a small gasp. We've been at this for 2 weeks now, and every gasp, every moan, every contented sigh is better than the last. I'm surprised we wrapped this draft up as quickly as we did, considering how much of our time has been spent on top of each other.

"We'll summon him tomorrow," she mumbles, breaking the bubble. I let out a heavy sigh, leaning my forehead against her stomach. *Damn it.* Then she hooks a finger under my chin, tilting my face to hers. "But tonight," she breathes. "I'm all yours."

In a feat of athleticism that I genuinely didn't think I possessed, I lift the backs of her thighs as I stand from my chair, wrapping her legs around my waist.

"Is that so?" I growl, and she nods. I walk her to the bed and drop her on her back in a fit of giggles.

She props herself up on her elbows, eyes locked on me and

full of hunger. I crawl on top of her, meeting her halfway as she yanks at my shirt collar and crashes her lips to mine. The familiarity of her touch is comforting, even as it heats my blood. I bring one hand up to cradle her face, the other supporting my weight as she slips my shirt up my back and over my head. I release her just long enough to toss it aside.

She arches her back just enough to pull my hoodie over her head. Is it even my hoodie anymore? Whatever. My brain ceases all rational thought when I see that the hoodie had nothing at all under it. I let out a groan at the sight and bury my face against her bare chest before trailing kisses up to her neck. She reaches down to slide her shorts off and I follow suit. I lean back and take her in again, like I do every time I have her like this.

"You are so fucking beautiful," I rasp, and her cheeks flush as if I don't tell her this every time, too. My head dips down, ghosting kisses along the swells of her breasts. I cup a hand around the outside of each, running my thumbs along the ridges of her nipples as they pebble under my touch. She arches her back under me, head tilting back. I skate one hand up the center of her chest and wrap my long fingers up the side of her exposed throat. My index finger hooks behind her teeth, holding her jaw open firmly. With nothing to muffle the sound, her moan echoes around the room.

My free hand drifts down to her center, finding her already dripping and ready. I groan as I swirl my middle finger around her clit, eliciting another moan from her. She bucks her hips, seeking more friction as I keep my movements torturously slow. She tilts her head down enough to level me with a glare and lets out an indignant whine around my finger.

"Relax, troublemaker," I tell her, gently sliding one finger inside her. "I'll get there." I pull back, pushing two fingers deep inside her on the next thrust, and she gasps. I continue pumping in and out of her slowly, adding my thumb to the mix. I can feel the tension building in her jaw, her walls tightening around my fingers. I dip my head down to wrap my lips around her nipple, following it with a quick bite. I release her jaw to wrap my hand fully around her throat, squeezing tightly at the sides as she squirms under me. Her body tenses, right on the edge, and I loosen my grip, letting the blood rush back to her head. Her eyes roll back, the hand flying up to cover her mouth barely muffling her as she screams my name.

At least the neighbors know who to bitch about.

I drop to the bed beside her, handing her the bottle of water from the nightstand that she didn't actually ask for. At this point, I feel like I can read her mind. I don't know if it's her magic or *our* magic or what, but she never has to ask, or correct, or even explain. I know I can project what I'm thinking about the book to her by accident, but it feels like we're so in tune with each other that the limitations on that bridge are gone.

Not just in bed, either. I find myself getting up to make her a cup of coffee that she didn't ask for at least once a day. When I'm having a hard time focusing because the TV is too loud, she turns it down before I can even reach for the remote. I have a craving for something and she poofs it into existence on the desk in front of me.

Something in the back of my brain tells me that I should be annoyed that she might be using her magic to get into my head, and I was at first. The more I think about it though, the more I really can't bring myself to hate it. She wants me to be happy. Comfortable. It's not like I'm not already obsessed with her to begin with, magic or not.

What I don't get, though, is how I'm hearing her, too. It's not like hearing her voice in my head. It's more like a feeling. Sometimes it's a flash of color accompanied by a taste or a smell, and I just kind of know. When I have her like this, some instinct just tells me exactly what she wants. It's like there's an invisible string connecting little cup phones in our heads, echoing our unspoken thoughts both ways down the line. It's how I know she's scared about tomorrow and needs a distraction.

It's how I know she's dying for me to bury my face between her thighs and devour her like she's my last meal right now, too. Of course, I oblige, and the sounds she makes are their own reward.

Chapter Fifteen

It's almost ten by the time I finally open my eyes. Callie is still fast asleep, her head cradled into my shoulder and her leg wrapped around mine. I gently untangle us, careful not to wake her, and slip out of bed. I start some coffee while I go through the grueling process of waking up. Once I'm at least 40% functional human, clad in sweats and an unbuttoned flannel, I quietly step out of the bedroom, pulling the door mostly shut so the noise doesn't wake her, and start on breakfast.

At this point, I've learned that Callie will eat literally anything, but a big breakfast spread is her absolute favorite meal. She did previously lead me to believe that it was tacos, but that was before I made her breakfast for the first time. Since today is the big day, I figured I'd go all out.

By the time she peeks her head around the door, the eggs and hashbrowns are almost done and the French toast, bacon, and sausage are warming in the oven. Her eyes light up at the sight and she practically bounces her way into her seat at the table. I pour a fresh cup of coffee and set it in front of her, leaning down to press a kiss to the top of her head from behind her chair.

"Good morning," I say, sliding a hand over her collarbone and squeezing gently.

"Good morning," she mumbles back over the mug that she's already holding to her lips. She takes a big gulp before tilting her head back and gracing me with a beaming smile. I lean down again, swallowing it up with another kiss.

We eat in easy silence, low music drifting from the speaker on the counter. When she's had her fill, she leans back in her seat and props her feet up on my lap. Her eyes drift closed, and she laces her fingers together, laying them across her stomach.

Of course, because I'm nothing but a ball of anxiety shaped like a person, I have to ruin the peace. I tap her foot, and she cracks one eye open in my direction.

"So, are we ready for this?" I repeat the question that I've asked her a thousand times over the last week. Her open eye narrows to a glare before she closes it again.

"Yes, Devon. We are ready for this," she says, her frustration clear in the enunciation of each word. "As ready as we can be."

I know I'm trying her patience at this point, but my need to be prepared for every situation is compulsory and this feels like a particularly important situation to be prepared for. She's assured me ad nauseum that we're as prepared as we can be to deal with Apollo because his erratic nature makes it impossible to predict what he'll do, but I can't help myself.

I decide to stop digging myself into a hole and wrap both hands around her feet, running my thumbs up the soles. Her head falls back, a faint smile making a reappearance, and I can see the annoyance on her face disappear. I'm lucky she's easy to please because I can be an incredibly taxing motherfucker sometimes.

"It'll be okay," she says quietly after a few minutes. "Worst case scenario, he takes me back." I start to object but she cuts me off. "If that happens, we'll find another way. I won't lose you forever." Her voice is resolute, like this is a foretold prophecy and not just her best guess, but I nod in agreement anyway. What else can I say?

"Is there anything you want to do before we leave?" *Just in case you don't come back?* I keep that part to myself.

She hums quietly, tapping a finger to her lips. "I don't think so. But do you think the gazebo will be crowded today? Maybe we could summon him there?"

"It's pretty cold today so I doubt anyone will be there. It's more of a spring and fall thing anyway." I hesitate for a moment, remembering who exactly we're meeting with. "He's not going to like... destroy the place, is he?" She barks out a laugh, but I'm not kidding. If he destroys one of the Seven Wonders before I get to take her there for a date, I'll be *so pissed*.

"No, probably not," she says, a bit too nonchalantly for my taste.

"*Probably?*" She shrugs, and my eye twitches. Today is going to fucking suck. I can feel it in my bones.

We procrastinate for another hour or so, cleaning up from breakfast and deciding what to wear. I'm standing shirtless in front of my closet, a button-down dress shirt in one hand and a hoodie in the other. Since I have no idea what this whole ordeal is going to entail, I have no idea how to dress or what to bring with me. Is he going to be offended if I don't dress nice enough? Or should I be dressed to run? Or fight? Before I can completely spiral, Callie wraps her arms around me from behind, her cheek pressed to my back. I drop the shirt I'm holding and fold my hands over hers, my head falling back with a heavy sigh.

"It'll be okay in the end," she whispers against my back. "And if it's not okay, then it's not over yet." I take a deep breath to calm my nerves and peel her hands away. I turn to face her and cup one hand around her cheek. Her eyes drift closed, and she sighs as she leans into my touch.

"I won't let him take you," I vow. "Not without a fight." She nods, and I hope she understands how deeply I mean it. I'll win her freedom for her, or I'll die trying. I can't go back to how things were before. Simply existing as I float through life, nothing more than a ghost who hasn't died yet. That's no longer an option. I'll spend the rest of my life with her, or I'll fucking haunt her. Either way, she's mine.

"He'll appreciate business casual, by the way," she tells me, plucking the black button down from the floor and holding it out to me. I pull the shirt on and start on the buttons, but they transform in my fingers. My plain cotton shirt shifts into some kind of silk blend, soft and shiny. It feels more expensive than anything I've ever worn.

"This is a little more business than casual, don't you think?" I raise an eyebrow at her, and she smirks at me before turning to rummage through my closet.

"Go big or go home," she says with a laugh, tossing an old blazer at me. I sigh as I slip it on over the shirt. She eyes me for a minute, her face scrunched up in concentration, and then the solid black polyester becomes a deep burgundy, silky like the shirt but with the thickness of wool. I hold a sleeve close enough to inspect the immaculate stitching and let out a low whistle.

I look down and realize my jeans have received the same treatment. "Hey," I shout in mock indignation. "These were my best jeans!"

She laughs and pats my chest, raising up on her toes to plant a quick kiss on my cheek. "Yes, they were, and that's a criminal offense. We'll get you better jeans tomorrow." She steps back and takes one last look at me before morphing her shorts and sweater into a formal dress. It's the same color as my blazer, sleeveless with a deep neckline that plunges down to her waist and held together by transparent mesh. The hemline lays just above her knees in the front and flows out a little longer in the back.

She steps over to the mirror on the back of the bedroom door and does a little twirl, her gaze analyzing. She looks around the room, snatching up one of her shirts and changing it into a black tweed coat. She turns back to the mirror and pulls the coat on, twisting around to see all the angles before nodding in approval.

"Okay," she says, huffing out a deep sigh. "I think we're ready." I nod, hoping I don't look as nervous as I am. *Well, at least one of us is ready.*

I follow her out the door and we head to the park. On the way, I realize that she mentioned "summoning" Apollo, but I think I'd remember if she did some kind of summoning ritual in my apartment, right?

"So, do we just do this summoning thing when we get there?" She looks at me like I've grown an extra head. Like *I'm* the weird one here.

"I texted him this morning," she tells me, laughing like I asked her if we were sacrificing a goat in the park. My jaw falls open. Apollo, Olympian God of the sun, light, art, and general shitheadery, has a fucking *cell phone*?

"Devon," she starts, trying to hide the smile in her voice and failing miserably. "What did you think I was doing to summon him?"

My cheeks flush, because the goat idea really wasn't far off from my original assumption. "I don't know," I mumble, shrugging. She sits back in her seat with a smug grin, because she's a *dick*. I think I might be rubbing off on her.

We pull into the main parking lot at the park and, as expected, there's no one else here. We walk up the cobbled path to the gazebo and Callie marvels at the winter landscaping. She runs her fingers carefully over the azalea bushes, stopping to admire the dormant blooms up close. The rose bushes are all pruned back for the season, but there's a wall of evergreens surrounding the area with a few sitting areas just inside the perimeter.

She strays from the path to admire an early bloom on a magnolia tree hanging over a bench, careful not to get close enough to anything that might dirty her dress. Luckily the ground is completely frozen. She waves me over to look at it and I can't help but laugh. I know she's actually enjoying herself, but I think she's stalling a little bit, too. *Fine by me.*

When we finally make our way to the previously empty gazebo, one of the benches is no longer empty. It's been in our view the entire walk up the path, but somewhere in between blinks, a man appeared out of thin air. Even sitting, I can tell he's huge. He has to be well over six feet tall. He's wearing a tailored black suit with golden cuff links and stitching, and I'm suddenly glad for Callie's makeover. He sits with one arm over the back of the bench, the other scrolling through the phone he holds on his lap. He doesn't even look up when he speaks.

"You're late," he drones, sounding incredibly bored, and I'm hit with a wave of irritation. As if he can feel it, he looks directly at me, eyes locking on mine in a sneer. His eyes are a shining, metallic gold, and his gaze is piercing. He's annoyed to even be here, and he wants me to know it. *Awesome.*

"We're not *late*," Callie argues quietly, hands clasped in front of her. She's wringing her fingers together nervously, but her voice is steady. "You're *early*." He stuffs his phone into the inside pocket of his jacket and turns his attention to her, lacing his fingers together and leaning forward on his knees. His gaze rakes over her from head to toe before he speaks, and I know I caught a flash of hunger in it.

"Early is on time, and on time is late. You know I hate to

be kept waiting. Why did you call me here?" He glances at me again in silent question. *And why is he here?*

His voice is deep and smooth, with an accent I can't quite place. Logically, it should be Greek, but it doesn't sound like any Greek accent I've ever heard. Maybe the accent morphed over the centuries, and this is *ancient* Greek. Either way, he sounds like an asshole. Callie clears her throat quietly before answering him.

"I want to bargain for my contract," she tells him, locking her violet eyes with his golden ones. He scoffs, arching one eyebrow in amusement. She narrows her gaze at him. "I want to know the cost to buy it out," she continues, trying to appear unfazed.

He leans back in his seat and drapes his arms over the back, and I'm overcome with a visceral need to kick him in the teeth just to wipe that look off of his face.

"And why, exactly," he drawls, dragging out the words. "Would you want to do a silly thing like that?" He turns his attention back to me, and we both know that he already knows the answer to his own question. He's just daring her to say it out loud. I stay silent, letting her take the lead and share only what she wants to, but I know he knows. And I know he's not happy about it. Callie steps closer to me, drawing his gaze back to her.

"Do my reasons matter? I no longer want to be bound to the muses, and he wants to buy my contract." She nods her head to me, but Apollo doesn't budge. "So, what's the price?"

Apollo is silent for a moment, glancing back and forth between us. It's the sly smirk of a plotting man, and it's making my skin crawl. After what feels like an eternity, he stands gracefully, making no noise at all. He's even taller than I thought, and his suit strains across his broad shoulders. A few steps close the gap between him and Callie, and he leans down so they're almost face to face. He hooks one finger under her chin and pushes until she can't help but look him in the eyes.

Instinct tells me to rip his hand off of her face, but logic tells me she'll ask for help when she needs it. I shove my hands in my pockets before I do something stupid and fuck everything up, but keep my eyes trained on hers for the smallest hint that things are not going as she had planned. She meets his cloying look with indignation, waiting for her answer.

"The price, sweet girl," he declares, his words dripping with the poison of a man who feeds on the suffering of others. "Is your immortal life."

Chapter Sixteen

"What the fuck," I sputter. "No." I take a step forward instinctively, but Callie stops me with a hand on my chest. I glance down at her, and she nods, the message loud and clear. *I've got this.*

"That makes no sense, Apollo." Her tone is bored, like his nonsense is grating on her patience. She's doing an excellent job of appearing more confident than she's feeling, but I'm willing to bet he can see through it. I turn my gaze back to him and his shit-eating grin confirms my suspicions. I'm sure she notices, too, but she doubles down.

"Why would the price for my freedom be my own life? You think I'd free myself just to die?" She rolls her eyes, as if the whole thing is beneath her. A waste of her time. The silence hangs heavy in the air, but she doesn't jump to fill the void. She just stares him down, arms crossed in annoyance.

"Well, you're welcome to bargain, of course." His gaze is predatory, and I want to light him on fire. I follow his gaze with mine as he traces her curves before dipping his head, eyes darkening. "I could always use another wife," he suggests with a wolfish smile. *That's it, motherfucker.*

I'm vibrating with barely controlled rage at this point, and she knows it. She uncrosses her arms and slips one hand into mine, squeezing hard. Of course, Apollo misses nothing. The delight on his face is absolutely infuriating.

"Oh my," he trills with a giddy laugh. "It seems there may be another chip on the table for you to bargain with? It's not worth as much as an immortal life, but I might be willing to accept his mortal one as payment instead."

That finally cracks the mask. She whips her gaze to him, fury burning in her eyes. "You will do no such thing," she grits out. He holds up his hands in mock surrender, stepping back and returning to his seat on the bench. He crosses his feet at the ankles and leans back, a wide smile splitting his face when he returns his gaze to hers.

"Doesn't seem to me like you have much else to bargain with." He brings one hand to his face, pretending to inspect his nails. Now *he's* playing bored. "You seem particularly overprotective of this one, Callie. Tell me, love. Does he know what happened to the last one?"

Her hand tenses in mine and she glances back at me. I catch a flash of shame on her face and shake my head. He's trying to drive a wedge, to create enough doubt that I'll back out, and I won't let him. Whatever happened, it has no real importance here. If it did, she would have told me. She's still frozen, and Apollo is loving every second of this. I decide that now is the time to take over.

"We're here to bargain, Apollo. A bargain benefits both sides in some way" His lip curls in a sneer at my voice, disgusted that I would dare to speak to him so informally. I resist the urge to roll my eyes. "Are you not willing to offer us a bargain worth taking?"

He's silent for long enough that I don't think he's going to bother answering me. He chews his cheek, like he's deciding what to say. When he finally speaks, it's to Callie.

"Tell him now, little bird. See if he still wants to fly away with you." He huffs out a laugh. She hesitates, turning to look at me but saying nothing. "Go on, or I'll take my leave. I tire of this."

She takes a deep breath and turns away from me. Her voice is so low that I almost don't hear her.

"My last charge was obsessed with me," she mumbles, fists clenching at her sides. "When I started the contract, I took the apartment next to his. I..." She stops for a moment, and I hear a telltale sniffle. I reach for her hand, but she pulls it away just as I make contact, cradling it with the other in front of her chest. "I kept making mistakes, and he connected the dots too quickly. He noticed he wrote better when I was around, and he worked out exactly what I am. I... I couldn't lie to him when he asked me, and I made the mistake of telling him I was only assigned to him until he finished his first book."

I'm immediately seeing red. I know exactly where this is going, and it's not going to end well for this piece of shit when I find him. She finally turns to look at me, silent tears streaming down her cheeks. My face crumples, and it takes every shred of control I have not to reach out for her again. I know she needs to get this out first, so I shove my hands in my pockets and give her an encouraging nod. She takes a deep breath before continuing.

"He... Well, he was a really good liar. He convinced me that we were friends, and I would come over to help him write." My brows knit together in a scowl, and I realize too late that she thinks I'm mad at her. Her face floods with panic, and she rushes to explain. "Not... not like us, I swear."

"Hey, it's okay." I shake my head, trying to reassure her. "I'm not mad, I promise. Not at you." She eyes me warily, chewing her bottom lip nervously. I do my best to soften my face, and some of the tension on hers fades away.

"Well, one day I came over to his apartment, and he made

us food. He thought I'd have some kind of mythical metabolism, I guess. He put way too much of whatever it was in my food, and I almost died." Her voice is so small at the last words, and I'm considering hunting the motherfucker down and offering him to Apollo.

"I didn't, though, obviously," she mumbles. "Anyway, I guess the friend he got the drugs from was also a nurse, and he came over to help keep me alive. When I woke up, he had me handcuffed to the radiator in his bedroom. He didn't do anything... weird..." *Right, except kidnap you.* "He just didn't want me to disappear once he finished his book. He didn't know that someone would come looking for me once the contract was up..." She trails off, her gaze drifting to Apollo.

"When our sweet girl here," he takes over, still talking directly to Callie. He's barely looked at me since we got here. "Didn't show up after his book had been published, one of the muses went to collect her and found her still chained up like a dog. We couldn't have that, of course. She called me right away, and I dispatched her little...*friend.*" He spits out the last word like it tastes bad, his lip curling in disgust. "With *extreme* prejudice."

Well, there goes my assassination plan. By the pleased look on Apollo's face, he's probably in little pieces scattered in every river in the country now.

They both turn their attention to me, obviously waiting for me to bail. Callie's watery eyes drift to the floor, and she lets out a low sigh.

"If you want to go, it's okay. I understand." Her voice shakes, and she rubs the heels of her palms over her eyes. My face contorts with fury, and I pin Apollo with a glare.

"Was that supposed to make me run?" I grit the words out, jaw clenched so tight my molars might break. Callie drops her hands, wide eyes locked on me in shock. "Did you think the actions of a weak piece of shit would make me think any less of her? That whatever punishment you doled out for his bullshit would scare me? I'm not bargaining for her freedom so I can use her for myself. If I thought for one second that I was capable of being the kind of man who would want her only for what she could do for me, I'd offer myself up to you right now, because I wouldn't deserve to live." His smirk has fallen into a deep scowl.

"I know this might be hard for you to understand, but I want her freedom so she can be *free*. Even if she uses that freedom to fly away without me. So, give me a *fair* bargain, or we'll figure out another way." *Fuck, probably shouldn't have thrown that last part in there. Whatever.*

He eyes me for a moment, eyes narrowed and analyzing. I've definitely pissed him off, but I'm hoping he's more impressed by my boldness. It's not lost on me that he could have killed me already and he hasn't.

Callie is still staring, unmoving. I hold out a hand for her, and her gaze drops to it for a moment before lacing her fingers with mine. My shoulders fall with relief at the contact. Both of our palms are clammy, and I can feel sweat dripping down the back of this ridiculous suit. I'm so fucking ready to take her home, take all this shit off, and curl up in bed.

"How sweet," Apollo says, eyes rolling with his words. We both turn to him, awaiting the result of his deliberation. "But the price remains the same. Her immortal life or your mortal one." My nostrils flare, fury flashing across my face. "Ah, ah," he tuts, his face full of amusement. "Before you try something crazy that will definitely get you *dismembered*," he warns, lifting an accusatory eyebrow at me. "Take the night to think about it. *Really* think about it. Meet me tomorrow with your decision. Same time, same place."

There's a loud pop and then he's gone.

"Fuck!" I kick at the bottom of the bench he was sitting on and achieve nothing but hurting my fucking foot, of course. Callie slowly sits down on a bench on the opposite side of the gazebo, staring straight through the spot he disappeared from. I take the seat next to her, pulling her into my arms and tucking her head under my chin. She immediately lets out a strangled sob, and I pull her in tighter.

"Shh, it's okay," I whisper, rubbing small, soothing circles on her back. "Fuck him. We'll find another way." She sniffs, and I press a kiss to the top of her head. "Come on, let's go home."

Chapter Seventeen

When we get back to the apartment, the first order of business is to strip out of thousands of dollars' worth of uncomfortable clothes. Callie offers to magic them back, but I decide to leave them. The decision has absolutely nothing to do with the way I caught her eyeing my ass in the car window on the way to the park, of course.

Once we're both clad in jersey and fleece, we curl up under the covers. I tuck her into me, cocooning her with her back to my front and my arms wrapped around her. We lay there like that in dark silence for a while, processing everything that happened before we figure out our next move. Finally, I gently pull my arm out from under her and plant a kiss on her temple before heading to the kitchen.

When I return with snacks and coffee for the brainstorming session, she's already scribbling in a notebook. I set the mugs down on the nightstand and plop down next to her. I peek at the notes she's written down so far, but they're impossible to decipher. They look like they're in another language, which I guess makes sense. I run my thumb over her bare knee, and she looks up at me.

"So, is there someone over his head who we can go to? Anyone who can overrule his shitty terms?" She purses her lips and shakes her head. Not an option, then. "Maybe one of the muses can help?"

"No, any of them who would be willing to help wouldn't be of any use, and anyone with enough power or authority would either turn me in to Apollo to garner favor and a spot on Helicon, or she wouldn't even understand why I would want to leave in the first place." She huffs, sliding the pen behind her ear and dropping the notebook on the bed. "The only one above him is Zeus and that's an even worse idea."

"Okay, what about a physical approach? Can we kill a god?" She actually laughs at that.

"No, Devon. We cannot *kill a god*. First of all, because they're immortal. Second of all, we are a mortal with minimal combat experience and a shitty muse with basic transfiguration powers."

"Right," I mumble. "Kidding, obviously." *Mostly kidding, anyway.*

"Honestly, I'm not that consequential. He has no reason to give a shit about me." She shrugs. Her tone is nonchalant, but I can feel the anxiety bubbling just beneath the surface. "Your book isn't officially published yet, so technically my current contract is still active. I think the best plan of attack is to show up tomorrow, tell him we changed our minds and to forget about it entirely, and then drag out the contract until we figure out a better plan."

"It's not a bad plan, but I think you're grossly underestimating his ability to be a petty piece of shit," I muse. She huffs, but she knows I'm not wrong. "I saw the way he looked at you. He might not have cared about you before, but now that you're on his radar as something he can't have, he wants to keep you." My nails dig into my palms at the memory of his slimy gaze dragging over her.

"Yeah, but he's also lazy. If I'm too difficult, he'll give up and find someone else to fuck with." Her wavering voice betrays her, and I know she doesn't believe her own words.

"Are you willing to bet on that?" I arch an eyebrow at her, and she chews on her bottom lip in lieu of a response.

"Well, I don't have any better ideas," she concedes with a sigh. "He's a *god*. We can't overpower him. My magic is barely a drop in the ocean compared to his. The best we can do is play meek, prey on his vanity, and tell him we've seen the light and he's absolutely right." She cringes at the thought and lets out a defeated sigh.

I pull her into me, cradling her in my lap. She melts into my grasp, and my chest tightens. There's no way in hell I'd be able to let them take her away. They'd have to kill me first.

Unfortunately, Apollo could, easily. And he would. *Happily*.

Callie nudges the top of her head against the bottom of my chin. I bring my hand up to cup her face, pressing it against my chest before trailing back to thread my fingers through her loose hair. Gently running my fingernails over her scalp, I lean back on the bed and pull her down with me.

It doesn't take us long to fall asleep like that, snacks and coffee and brainstorming forgotten. I wake up shortly after, just enough to drag a blanket over us, and immediately pass back out. When I open my eyes again, I know I'm dreaming because I'm in a dark cave. Water drips from the ceiling in a steady rhythm.

As my vision adjusts to the low light, I glance around the rough stone walls. I never could remember the difference between stalagmites and stalactites, but there are three of them sticking up out of the ground directly in front of me, and I could swear I saw one of them move. I squint at them, trying to bring them into focus, and have to swallow a scream when three horrifying mouths full of gnarled teeth become clear.

I rub my eyes and focus again, scrambling for my phone to shed some light on whatever the fuck is in front of me. Of course, I'm in a dream, so my phone is nowhere to be found. A tiny light appears in front of one of the figures, and I squint again until it's clear. A white taper candle floats in the air, its small flame illuminating the three figures. Their tattered hoods hide their faces from the nose up.

Their smiles aren't quite menacing, but they are definitely unnerving. What I can see of their faces is pale, probably from living in a fucking cave doing weird cave-dweller shit. The one on the left looks like a teenager, with smooth skin and a round face. Her right hand holds up one side of a piece of golden twine. In the center is definitely a middle-aged woman, the lower half of her sharp features illuminated by the flame. I realize that the candle isn't floating, but rather held in her outstretched, cloaked hand, the skin on her fingers so pallid it blends in with the white wax.

I don't know a ton about Greek mythology, but I know these have to be the Fates. Whether they're real or just my brain pulling all the information it has stored on the Greek pantheon and dumping it into my dream has yet to be determined.

The last figure, an old woman with deep wrinkles around her mouth and covering her fingers, holds the other end of the golden twine with her left hand, stretching it out in front of the three of them. They stare at it intently, as if they don't even see me here.

And then, all at once, their eyes trail from the twine to me. Their gaze feels like thousands of bugs crawling on my skin. Like it's unnatural to be making eye contact with them. My body shakes with an involuntary shiver as the one in the middle raises a thin, ghostly finger to point at me.

"He who knows too much and too little," she says, her otherworldly voice made up of layers like multiple people speaking different languages all at once. *Ouch.* I'd be offended if I wasn't about to shit my pants. "He who loves selflessly and gives freely. He stands against an unbeatable foe with an unbeatable ego."

The thread stretched in front of her is glowing bright enough to illuminate the cave now, and the woman in the middle raises a pair of golden scissors to it, opening them and hovering below with the thread poised between the blades. Is this supposed to be Apollo's lifeline? Do they think I'm somehow supposed to kill him?

They have entirely too much confidence in me.

Snip. She slices through the thread, but it doesn't fall. Hovering in the air, both pieces quickly turn black, the color bleeding out from the cut edges. All four of us watch the thread with rapt attention, though only three of us have any idea what the fuck is going on.

The second the blackness touches the ends of the rope in the other women's fingers, the cut edges start to fray in midair, knitting the raw fibers back together like they'd never been severed. From the newly uncut center, the black starts to fade out slowly, giving way to a bright lavender. It doesn't glow quite like the gold did. It's bright, almost pastel, and it looks like it's lit from within.

It looks like Callie's eyes.

The familiar tint spreads across the rope until all the black bleeds out, dripping from the rope like blood and staining the floor before them. The brightness dulls, leaving behind just the light bluish-purple coloring.

"What is lost in anger will bloom," the old woman on the right says. She has the same layered voice, but it's hoarse and feeble. "What is given in love will nourish."

"What... What does that mean?" All three hooded faces

snap to mine, the old fabric rustling from the sudden movement. The hoods lift just enough that I catch a glimpse of three sets of empty eye sockets, and it takes everything I have not to jump back. I'm not sure how they manage to convey this much sass without eyeballs, but it's like being chastised by three moms who aren't mad, just disappointed.

"We watch," the younger girl on the left says, her winsome voice less ethereal than the others. "We see and we know. We see in your heart, and we know you are true. Do not let us down. Put your faith in her." She glances down at the thread and back to me.

"Okay, I think I get what you're telling me. So, I need to tell Callie what you said, right?" I wait expectantly, but they leave my question unanswered. I'm not sure they're even breathing. "What if we meet with him and he just kills us both?"

In lieu of an actual answer or anything that could possibly be helpful, the woman in the middle simply parrots the younger one's words. "Do not let us down," she repeats, and the others drop the thread on the ground to let her walk past them. She stops a foot away from me. Up close, I can see that her skin is almost translucent, thin blue veins trailing along the skin. Her cloak hides most of her stringy black hair, but small tufts stick out around her neck.

She holds up a hand, jabbing one knobby digit at my face. I back away slowly as she hovers a finger at me, her jagged, yellowed nail dangerously close to my face. With a speed I don't think she could possibly possess, she jams her finger into my forehead, pushing me back so fast that I lose my balance and topple backwards into the shallow water on the cave floor behind me.

The second I touch the water, I'm blinded by a bright light. I squint while my eyes adjust and find the offending light is the nightstand lamp in my bedroom. Callie sits up on her knees at my side, hands on my shoulders trying to shake me awake. My hands snap up to wrap around her wrists, eliciting a startled scream from her.

"Oh, thank fuck," she breathes, cupping my face with both hands. "You were moaning like you were in pain and I couldn't get you to wake up. I thought... I was afraid he did something..."

Now that my eyes are semi-functional, I can see that she was panic crying. I reach up and swipe a thumb across each cheek, wiping tears away.

"Hey," I whisper, peeling her hands from my face and wrapping my own around them. "I'm okay. I just had a weird... dream?" Her eyebrows knit in confusion. "I thought it was a dream," I continue. "Maybe a nightmare. But now that I'm awake, I don't think it was. There were three women in this cave with this thick thread between them, and they were trying to give me advice that didn't make any sense."

A knowing look washes over her face. "The Fates," she says, nodding. "What did they tell you? The exact words, if you can remember."

"Okay, um..." I scoot back on the bed and sit up. "Well, first they said something about us facing an unbeatable foe with an unbeatable ego. Talking about Apollo, obviously. The thread was glowing gold, but then they cut it, and it turned black." Alarm flashes in her eyes, so I continue quickly.

"The cut edges came together though, like nothing ever happened. Then the whole thread turned this purple color, and they started with the riddles." She rolls her eyes like this is an irritating but completely normal occurrence. "'What's lost in anger will bloom,' and then something like 'What you give in love nourishes', I think? Then they told me to trust you, and not to let them down. No pressure though, right?"

Her face scrunches up while she considers the women's words. "Did they say anything else?"

"Uh, not really. The one told me that they're watching us, and they know I'm true, whatever that means. And then she shoved me back into the water and I woke up."

"The water? What water?" Her panicked face is about to send me into my own spiral.

"I don't know, it was just water on the floor of the cave. Is that bad?"

"It wasn't like... glowing or anything, right? Just water?"

"I don't think so," I tell her, questioning my own memory now. "Pretty sure it was just water."

She sighs in relief. "Okay, good. I don't know what would happen if they dropped you in the Styx. I don't think you'd have ended up back here, though."

"The... Styx?" It sounds familiar but I can't remember why that would be bad exactly.

"The Styx is the river you cross to get to the underworld," she explains. "I mean, it made Achilles invulnerable but he was a demigod so I have no idea what it would have done to you." While my brain buffers from that particular nugget of information, Callie settles back into bed.

"Anyway, it was probably just a dream," she continues, but she doesn't sound as convincing as she thinks she does. She drags me back down by my shoulder and curls up into my side, pulling the comforter up over us both. With her arm across my chest, legs tangled in mine, my body finally releases all the tension and it's not long before I'm out again.

Chapter Eighteen

I wake the next morning with my stomach in knots, despite Callie's usually calming presence at my side. She stirs shortly after I do, snuggling closer into my side. I bury my face in her hair and squeeze her tighter to me with a sigh.

As much as I'd like to pull the covers over us both and stay here forever, we've got shit to do. I press a kiss to her forehead and slip out of bed.

She comes out to the kitchen just as I set coffee and eggs on the table. We eat in silence, and I can feel the tension emanating off of her from across the table. She's building up the courage to say something, so I stay quiet and let her. Halfway through her second cup, she finally turns to me fully and takes a deep breath, sucking in all the air in the room with it.

"If something happens today," she begins, sitting on her hands to hide the shaking. "I... please don't be a hero."

"Hey, didn't we already cover this?" I keep my voice as light as I can, hoping I can ease her nerves. "I'm in it to win it, baby." I stretch my arm out across the table, palm up, and wait. She huffs out a tiny laugh and lays a trembling hand in mine,

"Ok, but seriously. If something... if *anything* happens to me, promise me that you won't get yourself killed over it. Just run, hide, whatever. Don't try and follow me down."

"I won't," I promise, lying through my teeth. I can tell she's got something up her sleeve, and I'm trying to trust her, but I'm not letting her throw herself to the wolves alone. "But only if you promise not to go where I can't follow." I finish my coffee in one gulp and wink at her over my cup. She scowls at me, but it loses all its bite when she tips her head down, giving me a predatory gaze through her lashes. Suddenly, I know exactly how to ease those nerves.

I stand and round the table, eyes locked on hers. I lean down to wrap my palms around the backs of her knees and haul her up against me. She loops her arms around my neck, and her lips find mine. I walk us toward the kitchen and prop her up on the counter, releasing her knees to step in between them.

"I promise," she lies, because how could she promise that? But now is not the time, and currently the right place is on my knees, so I bite down my protests and settle in for second breakfast.

Hours later, we're ready to meet Apollo again. Well, as ready as we can be.

"Don't forget," she stresses as we walk to the car. "Stick to the plan. Do. Not. Deviate." She punctuates her words with quick little claps that would be significantly more adorable if we weren't potentially headed to our deaths. "Do not go rogue. Do not improvise. Do not pass go, do not collect two hundred dollars. Stick to the plan."

She morphed our clothes into a new set of matching outfits. Today's theme is forest green, apparently. My suit looks relatively the same, but her dress today is testing my self-control. It's dark green silk, cut low in the front and lower in the back. The mesh straps hang off both shoulders, and there are slits up both thighs that reach dangerous heights.

When I don't respond, she stops walking to pin me with a glare. She plants one hand on her hip, and the position separates the fabric all the way up, straining it against her thigh. My eyes zero in on the bare skin, the faint bruises already forming from my fingertips this morning.

Suddenly, my suit is uncomfortably tight.

I drag my gaze back up to hers and nod. "Got it," I confirm, and her face softens. "Stick to the plan." She lays a hand on my cheek, and I lean down to meet her lips with mine, pulling her into me with a hand on her back.

"I promise, I got it," I assure her. "Come on, troublemaker. Let's go piss off a god."

The drive to the park is quiet, her hand resting on mine over the shifter. When we walk up to the gazebo, Apollo is already seated on the same bench in the same spotless suit. He scrolls through his phone again, clearly bored with this waste of his precious time that he insisted on in the first place. He doesn't even look up as we approach.

The plan is to appeal to his mercy, appear pathetic, make him lose interest in us, and go home safely to plot another day. Unfortunately, I simply cannot be trusted to keep my cool around this asshole. The way he looks at Callie, like she's an object that he can possess or some peon that he can command, makes my blood boil.

So really, the most important part of this plan is that I keep my hot-headed mouth shut.

I wasn't like this before her. I was calm, always level-headed. I never spoke out against anything or made any waves. Not because I was afraid to, but simply because I didn't *care*. I don't know when I went from living to simply existing or if it was a gradual degradation, but I was just barely floating through my life until she dropped into it.

I *care* now. I care about *her*, and caring about her woke up all of those dormant parts of myself that I had forgotten about. Not just the writing, either. I'm excited to wake up now that it means waking up next to her. As much as I love hiding from the world in my apartment with her, I want to take her out to fun places and experience the world together. I want to eat at fancy restaurants and walk through holiday displays with her while she marvels at all the decorations.

Before her, I can't remember the last time I actually wanted to even leave the apartment. To be honest, I can't remember the last time I wanted to wake up.

I really hope today wasn't the last day I get to be happy to wake up.

We stand in front of Apollo while he continues scrolling through his phone. I follow Callie's lead, hands behind my back in silence. Waiting to be addressed, as if he means anything. As if he deserves our reverence. My eye twitches but I keep my mouth shut.

Of course he looks up at us at that exact moment.

Apollo's lip curls. He definitely caught me. I've fucked this up before we even started and he's just going to kill us both and-

"Good morning," Callie greets him quietly, head bowed. His gaze snaps to her, and his grin becomes hungry. *Keep your mouth shut keep your mouth shut keep your mouth shut...*

"Good morning, my dear. What a lovely sight." His eyes roam hungrily over her dress, and I can practically hear him begging for x-ray vision. *Wait, does he already have x-ray vision?* Nope, not going there right now or I'll lose it, and he'll turn my insides into outsides.

She gives him a little bow, and I hate every second of this. She shouldn't have to pretend to respect this petty piece of shit

just so he forgets about us. She shouldn't have had to beg him for her freedom in the first place.

"We spent the night considering your offer. While we appreciate your kindness and generosity, we humbly decline. We would like to spend the time that we have left together on this assignment, and then I'll return to the muses for my next assignment. I was wrong to wish to be released from my duties. It's an honor to be considered-"

He interrupts her speech with a loud, barking laugh and my stomach drops. I know in this moment that we are well and truly fucked.

"Oh, my dear. What a performance! Bravo," he exclaims, clapping his hands together slowly. "Do you think I can't feel the contempt radiating off of you two in waves? Your pretty words don't hide your audacious intentions, sweet girl."

Her face falls at his words and she glances at me, begging for forgiveness with her eyes, before turning back to Apollo.

"Do you think I'm naive enough to believe that you would change your mind in one night? That you would just see the light and return home? I know that look. That sparkle in your eye, the invisible string that ties you two lovebirds together? The second you little creatures feel that tug to another, you lose all sense of reason." He stands up now, taking slow steps to close the distance between them.

"I've seen it before. Orpheus following that thread straight to Eurydice in the Underworld. Pyramus jumping headfirst into death like a fool, his beloved Thisbe following after him. Patroclus donning Achilles' armor and dying as nothing more than a distraction to save his love. Helen and Paris started a war that killed hundreds for their own selfish love."

He leans in close to her face, a finger trailing along her jaw. I might actually jump out of my skin.

"And here you two stand, convinced that I would just release you to live out your days with your mortal over something as trivial as *love*? You belong to me, sweet girl." He grips her jaw tight, and she winces when he jerks it up to meet his towering gaze.

How the fuck are we getting out of this?

She glares at him, taking in a deep breath before her face shifts into a saccharine smile. Her eyes narrow on him and when she speaks, it's dripping with unadulterated contempt.

"What would you know of love," she asks him with a scoff. "No one has ever loved you in your long, miserable life. Your father couldn't care less about you, and he'll probably kill you one day so you don't kill him for his throne. Your mother raised you out of duty, feeding your ego and inflating your sense of self-importance, and then dropped you off in Olympus the moment you were old enough to survive on your own." She spits her words at him with intent to maim, but his face is a stone mask.

"You couldn't possibly understand why I would want to be free to live and love as I please because you've never been able to prove yourself worthy of the love of another. You wouldn't know what it's like to be loved so wholly that it fixes your broken parts, because you're damaged beyond repair. The only person who loves you is *you*."

She spits the last word out like poison. Apollo is still staring at her, emotionless and silent, but I'm about to have a full-blown panic attack. I'm screaming at her in my head. *What the fuck are you doing, Callie? Are you trying to get us both killed? Are you giving up?*

Finally, terrifyingly, his mask cracks.

It starts as a huff. The corner of his lip tilts up, eyes narrowing on her. His eyes are cruel as he barks out a laugh that seems to never stop. When he throws his head back, instinct pushes me into action. I grab Callie's hand and yank her out of his reach, running for the stairs with her in tow.

Before I even make it to the stairs, my hand squeezes around nothing.

I spin around just in time to see Callie suspended a foot off of the ground, Apollo's hand outstretched like he's using the Force to hold her up. He squeezes his fingers into a fist, and, with a sickening crunch that I can feel in every cell in my body, Callie's neck twists at an angle that simply cannot sustain life.

All of the air whooshes out of my lungs and I crumple to the floor. I'm screaming, but I don't know if it's out loud or in my head. My forehead pressed to the floor is the only thing keeping me from sinking into the ground and disappearing altogether.

Apollo's black leather shoe appears next to my face, and I jump back before he can kick me, but he doesn't move. He just stares down at me, his grin dripping with malice.

"She was a hateful, ungrateful little bitch who didn't deserve your sacrifice or your mourning. You're better off without her," he says, his voice as cold as his words. I want to scream at him that he's wrong. I want to tell him that every word she hurled at him was true, but before I can even try, there's a pop and then he's gone.

It's over.

I scramble across the gazebo floor and lift her limp body into my lap. Her neck is bent at a horrifying angle, her body still warm but not for long. I let out a sob that shakes my whole body, smoothing her hair back so I can see her face before it starts to pale.

What do I even do? Do I call the cops? She has no identity, and they'll think I took her out here to kill her myself. Do I hide her now and come back to bury her under the cover of night? I'll end up getting myself caught hiding a body and definitely go to prison. Or will she just dematerialize or something? What happens to muses when they die? Do they return to wherever they live when they're not on an assignment? Do they-

Callie gasps as her eyes shoot open, emanating a purple glow. There are no pupils, but I swear she's staring at me.

"Callie?" I gasp, turning her face back and forth by her chin. "Are you-... No fucking way. Come on, troublemaker. Come back to me." I tap her cheek lightly with my fingertips and her eyelids flutter, the light flooding from them blinking on and off with the movement.

Slowly, she turns her head to face me, and I take my first real breath since her last. I lean forward and press my forehead to hers. When I feel her fingers tangle into my hair, the relief is visceral. I plant a kiss on her forehead just as it dawns on me that her neck was in two fucking pieces 30 seconds ago.

When I lean back to check the injury, I'm more surprised than I should be to find that she looks like nothing ever happened. The glow is fading, and her eyes are a normal *mortal* light blue now. I check her over, poking and prodding around her neck to see if there's any damage, but she just laughs at me.

I'll never take that sound for granted again.

"I'm okay, Devon," she insists, placing her palm flat on my chest. "I promise, I'm okay." She pushes out of my hold and sits up.

"I see that," I say, eyebrows knitting together. "But *how?*"

Chapter Nineteen

All I can do is stare.

A minute ago, she was gone. Her neck bulged with the snapped pieces of her spine, her skin quickly cooling. She was *gone*, and I would have gone down fighting Apollo if he hadn't disappeared like a fucking *coward*.

A coward. Who am I kidding? He would have turned me into a walking red mist before I took my first step. There was nothing I could have done to prevent this, and nothing I could do to Apollo in retaliation that wouldn't have ended in my complete evisceration. I'm basically useless in this fight, and I don't know why she would even-

"I'm alive because of you," she says, halting my spiral with a gentle hand on my cheek.

"What?" I'm sure I heard her wrong because I did nothing of any use.

"What is lost in anger will bloom," she recites, her hand drifting to her throat subconsciously. Her eyes find mine and I'm graced with a small smile.

"What's given in love will nourish," I mumble, repeating the last line of the Fates' riddle. I'd been rolling it around in my head since I woke up, trying to figure out what the hell it was supposed to mean, but I'd been so focused on figuring out how their words would keep her alive that I didn't stop to think that maybe they were just telling me to sit tight.

"They've been watching us," she explains. "The Fates. When we went back to bed after they came to you, they came to me too. They gave us each a part of the puzzle as a test." She slips her hand into mine. "We passed."

"More like *you* passed," I correct.

"No, *we* passed. Your test was whether you would tell me what happened and stick to the plan or if you'd go off half-cocked and try to be a hero. My test was..." Her gaze drifts to where Apollo had sat before he simply willed her out of existence, and I can see in her eyes that the experience will haunt her for a long time.

"Your test was standing up to him and trusting the Fates. *We* passed," I concede, pulling her back into me. "And Apollo thinks you're dead so we're off of his radar. There's one thing I don't get, though. What was with their whole show with the thread?"

She gives me a sad smile and plucks a pebble from between the floorboards of the gazebo, holding it out in the palm of her hand. She stares at it until she's squinting, but nothing happens. It takes me a second to realize that *nothing is happening*.

"Oh, baby..." I wrap my hand around hers, closing it around the pebble. "I'm so sorry."

"It's just magic," she says with a shrug. She's trying to brush it off, but I know she's devastated. "I can live without it. At least I'm alive, right?"

I squeeze her tighter to me. "Yeah, at least you're alive," I agree. My eyes burn at how close I was to losing her forever.

"His deal was that he would take my immortal life for my freedom. The Fates didn't like that he offered an unacceptable deal with no room for negotiation, so they made him keep his word. They told me he would do it, and they said the price of his cheating would cost him. When he killed me, I lost my immortal life and won my own freedom, but they added a mortal core to my thread."

My mouth falls open as the pieces all click together.

"He burned away my immortality - and my magic - and left me with a mortal lifespan." She drops her gaze to the ground. "A mortal lifespan that may or may not be tied to yours."

My eyebrows shoot up at that. "What... what exactly does that mean?"

She squirms in my lap, wringing her fingers together like she's delivering bad news.

"Well, in order to give me a mortal lifespan, they had to... anchor it to something to keep it in the mortal realm, I guess? The Fates don't really make a habit of explaining themselves. When they appeared to me, they had another thread in front of them. It wasn't mine, and I'm guessing it was yours. They plucked a strand from it and fused it with mine. I thought they were telling me that they were reinforcing my thread to fight him or something, but I realized this morning that the riddle they gave you..."

"What's given in love will nourish..." I mutter under my breath, frozen by the realization. "They gave you a piece of my thread because yours needed a mortal core to survive. It *nourished* your thread."

She nods slowly, relief washing over her face as my smile grows. "So basically, you're stuck with me forever," she says with a nervous laugh. "Hope you're cool with that."

"Are you fucking kidding me?" Her face falls for a second at my words. I grab her chin and drag it back to me. "That's the best news I've ever heard," I beam. She lets out a relieved sigh and wraps her hands around the back of my neck, dragging me down to her lips.

We lose ourselves in each other for a while, marveling at the fact that we're both even alive, let alone free. My legs go numb, and I couldn't care less. Eventually, the cold sets in and we both start to shiver. I scoop her up and try to stand, forgetting that *both legs are numb, you idiot,* so we don't even make it off the ground.

Callie laughs at me for a solid minute, and I'm not even mad about it. How am I supposed to be mad about anything for the rest of my life when I get to spend it with her?

She stands, brushing off her dress and holding out a hand to me. I take it, bracing the bulk of my weight on the bench seat behind me so I don't yank her back down.

"Come on, troublemaker," I tell her, wrapping my arms around her waist and pulling her into me. "Let's go home."

Epilogue

It took six months to finish editing my book and get it picked up by a publisher. After that, it was a whirlwind of promotion photo shoots and then book signings and meet and greets. *Troublemaker's Ballad* drew so much interest before it was even released that events were sold out as soon as they went live.

We were booked solid 5 days a week for two months. Callie came with me to everything, of course. As it turns out, she not only had the foresight to use her magic to fabricate herself a new identity and all the documents to match it the night before our first meeting with Apollo, but also transfigured a nice stack of cash for us to live on until royalties started to come in. All it cost me were a few old books.

We took a break in the fall to visit the rest of the Seven Wonders. We picked apples and pumpkins on the farm and bought a bag of fresh corn and peas for the ducks on the trail. Callie hid a bag of treats in her pocket for our trip to the dog park, of course. We ran into Brendan's wife and her gigantic moose of a dog there, both of whom Callie was instant best friends with. Well, his soon-to-be *ex*-wife, anyway. She started painting again, and she looked happier than ever. Good for her.

It was warm enough to eat on the patio, so we stopped at the Mexican restaurant on the way to visit Callie's cow friends. They were closed to the public, but they were willing to make an exception for their new hometown celebrity. We skipped the gazebo and opted for an encore at Strikers.

Almost a year later, we're holed up in a cabin in the mountains while I work on the sequel. As soon as Callie was officially free, I asked her what she wanted to do with the rest of her life. "Live it," she said. So, as soon as it was time to start writing again, we hopped on a plane and haven't stopped moving, exploring, and experiencing the world since.

I wasn't sure what would happen when Callie lost her powers, so I wrapped the story up nicely but also left it open for more. I'm working on the final chapter when she sets a cup of coffee in front of me, wrapping her hands around my shoulders and burying her face in my back.

"How much more?" she asks, nodding her head towards the open laptop in front of me.

"Another thousand words or so, I think. A few hours," I estimate, taking a sip of coffee.

"Would a break help? Or are you hyperfixated?" I check my watch, surprised to find that I've been writing since breakfast, which was *four hours ago*, without so much as a blink break.

This is how she helps me now. Of course, she still inspires and analyzes everything I write, but she also keeps me from burning myself out. It's funny that she spent hundreds of years as an immortal being, and now she's the one who reminds me that I'm basically a houseplant with a nervous system and need to do things like drink water and stretch and touch grass.

She's dealing with losing her magic much better than I thought she would. Much better than I would have for sure.

She still catches herself trying to use it sometimes, and what used to cause tears now makes her laugh. Occasionally, I'll find her deep in thought, her brain working overtime to force her into a spiral of inadequacy. I remind her regularly that she's equally amazing with and without powers. Sometimes it's enough to stop the spiral, sometimes not. It gets better every day, though.

She still wakes up gasping, clawing at her once-broken neck sometimes. One day I'll find a way to make Apollo pay for that.

For now, I'm just happy that she's free, and she's mine, and I'm hers.

It's also nice to know that my ability to write wasn't solely due to her muse influence. Sure, it made everything happen a little faster, but my publisher has the first half of the book already and they're saying it's even better than the first. If they're right and this blows up like the first one did, I've got a whole series plotted out and ready to be written.

I consider her question, debating whether I want to risk losing momentum. Her raised eyebrow makes the decision for me.

"You know what? Yeah, let's go lay by the fire." She bounces on her feet with a giant grin, and I suddenly couldn't give a fuck less about the book. I take her outstretched hand, and she leads me out the back door to the giant hammock in front of the fire.

With my body wrapped around hers, the heat from the fire warming us and the sounds of the forest filtering in through crisp autumn leaves, it's not long before we both doze off.

This is it. This right here is Heaven, or Elysium, Nirvana, Valhalla, or whatever brand of paradise you subscribe to. This is my paradise, and I'll savor every moment until I step into the next life with her hand firmly clasped in mine forever.

Acknowledgments

Boy, was this a wild ride. So many people were integral in this process, some without even knowing.

Mom, who encouraged every depraved bit of self-expression through every obnoxious phase of life.

Óst min, the inspiration for every swoon-worthy quote I write.

Kyra, my forever bestie, concert partner, personal nurse, ADHD co-handler, and spawner of my favorite shitlings.

Dani, my hype girl, my biggest cheerleader and my forever sounding board for all of my insane ideas.

Lise and Rosie, the best alpha readers on the planet, and my first review and pre-orders. Your eagle eyes and critical analysis made all the difference, and I appreciate you both so much.

My beta and ARC teams, for reading, reviewing, and taking the time to fall in love with Devon and Callie with me.

My Wallflowers and my Heathens, for your unconditional love and support from start to finish, and for indulging my insanity on a daily basis.

About the Author

Author portrait by @teoctobart

Layla Nox is an author of urban fantasy and dark romance from Ohio. She loves to explore worlds filled with magic and morally gray characters, drawing inspiration from her love for all things dark and spooky. When she's not writing, she can be found reading, playing video games, or working on a new craft project. *Marginally Yours* is Layla's debut novel.

Social Media
   Instagram/Threads: @laylanoxauthor
   TikTok: @laylanoxauthor
   Facebook: Layla Nox (@laylanoxauthor)

www.ingramcontent.com/pod-product-compliance
Lightning Source LLC
LaVergne TN
LVHW041951070526
838199LV00051BA/2988